新视角电影英语
New Perspective
成长篇

罗振宁　谭慧　主编

CFP 中国电影出版社

2011·北京

编 委 会 名 单

主　编：罗振宁　谭　慧

编　委：(以姓氏拼音为序)

　　　　鲍　雪　邓晓娥　刘　丽

　　　　莫　琳　庞亚平　宋雁蓉

前　言

**新视角电影英语
成长篇**

　　本套教材旨在以原版的英文电影为语言学习平台,通过运用故事性兼趣味性强的电影片段构建真实自然的英语语言学习环境和学习气氛,训练学生的语言听说能力,同时兼有阅读和写作的综合信息输入。在信息输入层面,本教程采用多样化的信息输入手段,即听觉信息和视觉信息,包括声音、图像和文字,通过灵活实用的方式不断提高学生捕捉获取信息的能力。在信息输出层面,首先,通过各种互动性口语表达训练,在学生理解电影片段内容的基础上,进行拓展性补充阅读,精选若干篇与影片内容有关的阅读文章,包括主要演员生平、影评和文化差异等,以此提高学生的阅读兴趣、提高学生的阅读水平;其次,提炼有文化内涵的各种不同话题,组织学生进行讨论或以电影片段为基础进行角色扮演来强化学生的听说技能;最后,通过形式多样的实用型写作练习提高学生的写作技巧和能力。

教材特色
　　本套教材是以精选的电影片段的台词作为

学生学习的重点内容来提高学生听、说、读、写等应用交际能力的基础性英语教材。根据所选电影主题的不同,全教材共分四册,分别是爱情篇、社会篇、成长篇和史诗篇。每册设五个单元,有如下特点。

1. 真实化:通过电影掌握以英语为母语人群的日常常用口语句型,并通过电影情节理解其句型的适用语境。

2. 立体化:从输入呈现、训练活动到交际输出,不断刺激学生学习英语的主体意识、思想和表达,充分体现了语言输入、信息传递、知识接受和文化融合的立体化。

3. 完整化:让学生了解正式语言与非正式语言、口语与书面语的区别。

教材的具体实施

1. 课文导入:讲授本章影片的故事梗概。

2. 精听训练:旨在提高学生的听力技巧和听力理解能力。

3. 会话训练:结合该课内容,设计多种课堂活动,包括角色扮演、对白模仿等帮助学生循序渐进地提高口语表达能力。

4. 语法知识:教师讲授基本知识点,通过让学生进行操练帮助学生熟悉并掌握英语基本语法知识概念。

5. 文化背景导入:教师讲授与该课有关的文化背景知识,包括电影拍摄幕后制作花絮、影片的主要演员经历、导演阐述等。

6. 练习设置:通过听说等活动,巩固本课所学,完成语言记忆和吸收,达到交际目的。

7. 第二课堂:该环节的设置是该课内容的延伸和补充。通过各种音像资料和各种趣味性活动强化学生的学习兴趣,拓展学生的知识面。

教材结构、目的和教学建议

教材结构	目的	课堂组织	建议时间
1. 预热练习	①影片及其背景知识介绍。②帮助学生回顾影片故事线索和主要情节,提示学生在该片中要碰到的真实生活场景。	活动形式:全班或分组。课堂组织:根据影片内容和故事发展,教师向学生提问与影片有关的话题,可以每个问题请一个同学回答,也可以在课堂内巡视学生的讨论情况。	15分钟
2. 影片对白	①遵循精听和泛听结合的原则,练习抓大意和抓细节的能力。通过较真实的言语输入让学生了解初次见面等真实生活场景所要用到的语言,引发学生思考在解决真实生活问题时需要运用哪些知识和判断。②影片片段提供语言信息的视觉输入,让听力较弱的学习者将听觉输入和视觉输入结合起来,加深语言在记忆中的印迹。	活动形式:全班。课堂组织:教师播放影片片段,学生自己在稿纸上写下对白的关键词。	每个场景30分钟
3. 语言点注释	①解释对白中的关键词汇和短语。②补充日常生活交际中所需要的词汇。③适当补充电影类型词汇。	活动形式:全班。课堂组织:教师讲解概念比较复杂的词或词组。	30分钟
4. 听力训练	遵循重复的原则,帮助学生重复练习以掌握语言重点,这是成功完成角色扮演和情境模拟的前提,有利于较为内向的学生降低焦虑度。	活动形式:双人或多人。课堂组织:教师选取典型的场景让学生填空。	10分钟

教材结构	目的	课堂组织	建议时间
5. 角色扮演	遵循模仿的原则,让学生进入真实的角色来使用语言,不仅感受角色的语言魅力,同时和现实交际任务结合起来,实现从形式到功能的转变。	活动形式:双人或多人。课堂组织:让学生按角色来扮演,教师鼓励学生从角色出发,充分体会到重点句式的必要。教师需要纠正发音方面的错误。	30 分钟
6. 阅读和写作	①根据影片内容,提供足够的额外信息,方便学生在课外进行相关知识的积累和相关话题的沟通。②配合介绍关于自然科学的 Discovery Channel Video 及 National Geographic Video 等系列片,这类影片的旁白(narration)并不像一般对话那样随性,而比较像是一篇文章,因此句子比较长,文法也比较复杂,教师可以讲解优美的句型结构,学生从中既可以提高阅读水平同时又可以学习写作技巧。	活动形式:单人或多人。课堂组织:自主学习。	学生自己掌握

教材使用对象

本套教材适用于大学非英语专业学生或同等程度的英语学习爱好者,同时也可以作为电影专业学生的参考教材或辅助教材使用。

本套教材在编写过程中曾得到北京电影学院教务处薛文波处长、基础部主任叶远厚教授的大力支持与帮助,在此,我们一并表示衷心的感谢。

由于时间急迫,书中的缺点和错误在所难免,我们诚挚地希望读者批评指正。

Contents

目录

Chapter One

Shrek

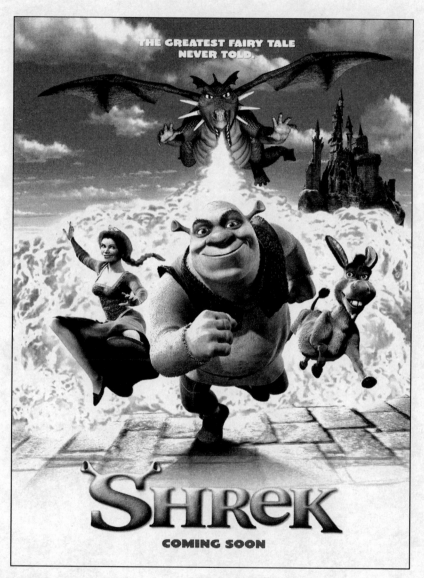

Sometimes things are more than they appear.

Main Characters
(Actors are listed for their voices)

Shrek.............................Mike Myers
Donkey.............................Eddie Murphy
Princess Fiona ....Cameron Diaz
Lord Farquaad.......................John Lithgow

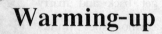

Warming-up

Synopsis

One day Shrek meets Donkey, a fast-talking and funny animal, and soon after, Shrek's isolated life is turned into chaos when hundreds of fairy tale beings invade his swamp. Donkey explains to Shrek that Lord Farquaad, of the distant land of Du-Loc, probably forced the creatures on to his land, and thus Shrek and Donkey head for Farquaad's castle to  try and get back his life of peace and quiet. After arriving at Farquaad's castle, Shrek agrees to try and rescue the beautiful Princess Fiona from the castle where she is living, trapped by a fire-eating dragon (a giant snake-like monster with wings). Farquaad wants to marry Fiona so he can legally become King of DuLoc, and thus he tells Shrek that if he brings him the

 Princess, he will force the fairy tale characters out of his swamp. Soon after, Shrek and Donkey head off to rescue Fiona. They free Fiona from the dragon, and all three are soon on their way back to Farquaad's

castle. Fiona seems particularly eager to get back and marry Farquaad, who she thinks must be her "true love." But the princess seems to have a dark secret, and Shrek and Donkey are not so sure that Farquaad is really the man for her. Once back at the castle, the wedding is about to take place, but then Fiona's secret is revealed, and Shrek, the ugly green monster, learns that he really doesn't want to live alone for the rest of his life, if he himself could find his own true love.

New Words

isolated ['aisəleitid]
adj. ① separate; single or unique 隔离的；单独的 ② standing alone; solitary 孤立的；孤独的

swamp [swɔmp]
n. (area of) soft wet land; marsh 湿软土地；沼泽

chaos ['keiɔs]
n. complete disorder or confusion 混乱；紊乱

invade [in'veid]
v. ① enter (a country or territory) with armed forces in order to attack, damage or occupy it 武装进入

（一国或一领地）；侵犯②interfere with sth. 干扰

distant ['distənt]　　　　*adj.* far away（in space or time）（空间或时间）远隔的；遥远的

capture ['kæptʃə]　　　　*v.* take sb. /sth. as a prisoner 俘获某人/某物

trap [træp]　　　　*v.* keep（sb.）in a place from which he wants to move but cannot 使（某人）陷入困境

particularly [pə'tikjʊləli]　　　　*adv.* especially 尤其；特别地

reveal [ri'viːl]　　　　*v.* ①make（facts, etc.）known 使（事实等）显露出来②cause or allow sth. to be seen 展现或显示

Phrases and Expressions

turn into：pass from one condition or state to another one 由一种状况转为另一种状况

head for：move towards（a place）向（某处）行进

take place：happen 发生

Discuss with your classmates and give answers to the following questions.

1. How do you describe Shrek?
2. What does Shrek look like?
3. Why does the Lord Farquaad want to marry Fiona ?
4. What's the secret of Fiona ?
5. What does Shrek do at the wedding of Fiona and Farquaad?

Scene Study

Scene 1

Shrek and Donkey head off to rescue Princess Fiona.

Fiona: You did it. You rescued me! You're amazing. You're... you're wonderful. You're... a little unorthodox I'll admit. But thy deed is great, and thine heart is pure. I am eternally in your debt. And where would a brave knight be without his noble steed?

Donkey: All right, I hope you heard that. She called me a noble steed. She thinks I'm a steed.

Fiona: The battle is won. You may remove your helmet, good Sir Knight.

Shrek: Uh, no.

Fiona: Why not?

Shrek: I... I have helmet hair.

Fiona: Please. I wouldn't look upon the face of my rescuer.

Shrek: No, no, you wouldn't...

Fiona: But how will you kiss me?

Shrek: What? That wasn't in the job description.

Donkey: Maybe it's a perk.

Fiona: No, it's destiny. Oh, you must know how it goes. A princess locked in a tower and beset by a dragon is rescued by a brave knight, and then they share true love's first kiss.

Donkey: Hmm? With Shrek? You think... Wait. Wait. You think that Shrek is your true love?

Fiona: Well, yes.

Donkey: You think Shrek is your true love!

Fiona: What is so funny?

Shrek: Let's just say I'm not your type, okay?

Fiona: Of course, you are. You're my rescuer. Now... now remove your helmet.

Shrek: Look. I really don't think this is a good idea.

Fiona: Just take off the helmet.

Shrek: I'm not going to.

Fiona: Take it off.

Shrek: No!

Fiona: Now!

Shrek: Okay! Easy. As you command, Your Highness.

Fiona: You... you're a... an ogre.

Shrek: Oh, you were expecting Prince Charming.

Fiona: Well, yes, actually. Oh, no. This is all wrong. You're not supposed to be an ogre.

Shrek: Princess, I was sent to rescue you by Lord Farquaad, okay? He's the one who wants to marry you.

Fiona: Then why didn't he come rescue me?

Shrek: Good question. You should ask him that when we get there.

Fiona: But I have to be rescued by my true love not by some ogre and his— his pet.

Donkey: So much for noble steed.

Shrek: Look, princess, you're not making my job any easier.

Fiona: I'm sorry, but your job is not my problem. You can tell Lord Farquaad that if he wants to rescue me properly, I'll be waiting for him right here.

Shrek: Hey! I'm no one's messenger boy, all right? I'm a delivery boy.

Fiona: You wouldn't dare. Put me down!

Shrek: Ya comin', Donkey?

Donkey: I'm right behind ya.

Fiona: Put me down, or you will suffer the consequences. This is not dignified! Put me down!

New Words

rescue [ˈreskjuː]	v. save or bring away sb. /sth. (from danger, captivity, etc.) （从危险、囚禁等中）搭救某人/某物
amazing [əˈmeiziŋ]	adj. surprising 令人吃惊的
unorthodox [ˈʌnˈɔːθədɔks]	adj. not in accordance with what is orthodox, conventional or traditional 非正统的；非传统的
admit [ədˈmit]	v. recognize or acknowledge sth. as true, often reluctantly; confess sth. 承认；供认
eternally [iˈtɜːnəli]	adv. throughout all time; forever 永远地；永久地
steed [stiːd]	n. horse 马
description [disˈkripʃən]	n. saying in words what sb. /sth. is like 对某人某事物的描述
destiny [ˈdestini]	n. power believed to control events 命运
command [kəˈmɑːnd]	n. order 命令
ogre [ˈəugə]	n. ① (in legends and fairy stories) cruel and frightening giant who eats people （传说和童话中的）吃人巨妖

②very frightening person 极可怕的
人

expect [iks'pekt]　　　　　　　*v.*　think or believe sth. will happen
or that sb. /sth. will come 预计；
预料

properly ['prɔpəli]　　　　　　*adv.*　in a proper manner 适当地；恰
当地

messenger ['mesindʒə]　　　　*n.*　a person carrying a message 送信
者；报信者

suffer ['sʌfə]　　　　　　　　*v.*　① feel pain, discomfort, great
sorrow, etc. 感到疼痛、不适、悲
伤等② experience or undergo（sth.
unpleasant）经历或遭受（不愉快之
事）

consequence ['kɔnsikwəns]　　*n.*　a result or an effect of sth. 结
果；影响

dignify ['dignifai]　　　　　　*v.*　make honorable 使有尊严、崇高

Phrases and Expressions

be in your debt：feel grateful to sb. for his help, kindness, etc. 欠某人之
情

take sth. off：remove (an item of clothing) from one's body 从身上除掉、
脱下（衣物等）

be supposed to do sth.：be expected or required to do sth. 本来或应该要做
的事

put sth. down：place sth. on a table, shelf, etc. 把某物放到桌子、架子等
上

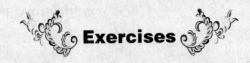 **Exercises**

 Comprehension of the Scene

Watch the scene carefully and tell if the following statements are TRUE or FALSE according to the scene you watched.

1. Fiona thinks Shrek is a very traditional type of rescuer who likes a prince.

2. Fiona takes Donkey for a noble steed.

3. Fiona asks Shrek to take off his helmet and Shrek can't wait to do so.

4. Shrek doesn't expect Fiona to kiss him and feels very excited.

5. Donkey feels very proud of himself to be called a noble steed.

6. Fiona is quite surprised and disappointed to realize that Shrek isn't prince charming.

7. Shrek also believes that Fiona is his true love.

8. Fiona can't wait to go back with Shrek and Donkey.

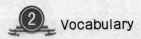 Vocabulary

Fill in the blanks with the words or phrases given below，and change the form when necessary.

remove	admit	properly	suffer
delivery	take off	rescue	be supposed to do

1. This poor old lady _____ from the loss of her husband and her son last year.

2. Would you like to _____ your wet jacket so I can dry it for you?

3. The police _____ the businessman in only 12 hours after he was kidnapped by some criminals.

4. The villagers _____ that big rock from the road and now they can drive through the road.

5. It's so surprising that Susan is dating a _____ boy from Pizza Hut.

6. You should _____ it if you have made a mistake on this project.

7. This foreign student cannot speak Chinese _____ as he has just started learning it.

8. People _____ pay tax for their personal income.

3 Further Study

Translate the following sentences into English with the words or phrases given in the brackets.

1. 请把这个婴儿放下来，否则他会受伤的。(put down)

2. 她把丈夫送给她的那枚钻戒锁起来，作为永久的纪念。(eternal)

3. 希拉里·克林顿是位非常了不起的政治家。(amazing)

4. 根据你的描述警察很快就抓到了小偷。(description)

5. 很抱歉，我不能嫁给你，因为你不是我喜欢的那种类型。(type)

6. 客人们已经等了近一个小时，那位明星还是没有到。(wait for)

7. 汤姆和罗斯相爱了，大家都认为是命运安排他俩相识的。(destiny)

8. 他由于缺乏经验而无法成为这次战争的信使。(messenger)

Scene 2

Shrek，Donkey and Princess Fiona head back to Farquaad's castle.

Donkey：Hey，can you tell my future from these stars?

Shrek： Well，the stars don't tell the future，Donkey. They tell stories. Look，there's Bloodnut，the Flatulent. You can guess what he's famous for.

Donkey：All right，I know you're making this up.

Shrek： No，look. There he is，and there's the group of hunters running away from his stench.

Donkey：That ain't nothin' but a bunch of little dots.

Shrek：You know Donkey, sometimes things are more than they appear. Hmm? Forget it.

Donkey：Hey, Shrek, what we are gonna do when we get our swamp anyway?

Shrek：Our swamp?

Donkey：You know, when we're through rescuing the princess that stuff.

Shrek：We? Donkey, there's no "we". There's no "our". There's just me and my swamp. The first thing I'm gonna do is to build a ten-foot wall around my land.

Donkey：You cut me deep, Shrek. You cut me real deep just now. You know what I think? I think this whole wall thing is just a way to keep somebody out.

Shrek：No, do ya think?

Donkey：Are you hidin' something?

Shrek：Never mind, Donkey.

Donkey：Oh, this is another one of those onion things, isn't it?

Shrek：No, this is one of those drop-it and leave-it-alone things.

Donkey：Why don't you want to talk about it?

Shrek：Why do you want to talk about it?

Donkey：Why are you blocking?

Shrek：I'm not blocking.

Donkey：Oh, yes, you are.

Shrek：Donkey, I'm warning you.

Donkey：Who you trying to keep out? Just tell me Shrek.

Shrek：Everyone! Okay?

Donkey：Oh, now we're gettin' somewhere.

Shrek：Oh! For the love of Pete!

Donkey：What's your problem? What you got against the whole world anyway?

Shrek：Look, I'm not the one with the problem, okay? It's the world that seems to have a problem with me. People take one look at me and go, "Aah! Help! Run! A big, stupid, ugly ogre!" They judge me before they even know me. That's why I'm better off alone.

Donkey: You know what? When we met, I didn't think you was just a big, stupid, ugly ogre.

Shrek: Yeah, I know.

New Words

block [blɔk]   v. prevent sb. /sth. from moving or progression 阻挡某人/某事物

judge [dʒʌdʒ]   v. form an opinion about sb. /sth. 判断某人/某事物

Phrases and Expressions

tell... from...: distinguish... from 从中辨认……

make up: ①invent sth. (esp. in order to deceive sb.) 捏造、虚构某事（尤指为欺骗某人）②compensate for sth. 补偿；弥补

a bunch of: group of people ; gang 人群；匪帮

 Exercises

 Comprehension of the Scene

Watch the scene carefully and tell if the following statements are TRUE or FALSE.

1. Both Donkey and Shrek believe that the stars can tell the future.

2. Shrek tries to tell Donkey to judge things from their appearance.

3. Donkey thinks that Shrek is against the whole world.

4. Shrek believes that nobody likes him even before they get to know him.

5. Very few people believe that Shrek is stupid and ugly.

6. Shrek wants to bring Donkey back to where they come from.

7. Shrek thinks maybe it's better for him to live alone.

8. Donkey also thought Shrek was stupid and ugly.

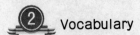 Vocabulary

There are four answers for each of the following sentences. Choose the correct one based on the scene you watched.

1. It's a bit hard to tell a person's character just _____ the way he or she speaks.

   A. in   B. with   C. from   D. on

2. She is better _____ divorcing her husband as he never cares about her.

   A. /   B. off   C. of   D. than

3. Don't take what I said too seriously. I just made it _____.

   A. up   B. of   C. /   D. off

4. What are you talking _____? I don't believe you.

   A. with   B. about   C. of   D. for

5. He seems to have a problem _____ all his colleagues. None of them likes him.

   A. about   B. of   C. at   D. with

6. This lady is famous _____ her children's stories. Many children know her name.

   A. for   B. with   C. about   D. upon

7. Some people like to judge a person _____ they even know him. This is wrong.

   A. when   B. after   C. upon   D. before

8. The dog ran _____ the hunter as soon as he appeared. The dog was

afraid of his gun.

    A. away with   B. with away   C. along for   D. along with

 Further Study

Translate the following sentences into English with the words or phrases given in the brackets.

1. 这个有经验的警察很快对形势作出了判断。(judge)

2. 我觉得你离开这个城市是明智的，因为它太小了，工作机会很少。(better off)

3. 我再次警告你，不许再和我的女儿约会了。(warn)

4. 在他们的婚礼上汤姆送给新娘一大束鲜花。(a bunch of)

5. 这个小孩非常善于编织各种借口。(make up)

6. 你为什么从那个女孩身边逃走？难道你不喜欢她吗？(run away from)

7. 布拉德·皮特凭借电影《七宗罪》出名。(famous for)

8. 他的外表和他的举止非常不一致。(appearance)

Scene 3
Princess Fiona starts to show kindness to Shrek.

Fiona：   Good morning. How do you like your eggs?

Donkey：   Good morning, Princess!

Fiona：   What's all this about? You know, we kind of got off to a bad start yesterday. I wanted to make it up to you. I mean, after all, you did rescue me.

Shrek：   Uh, thanks.

Fiona：   Well, eat up. We've got a big day ahead of us.

Donkey：   Shrek!

Shrek：   What? It's a compliment. Better out than in, I always say.

Donkey：   Well, it's no way to behave in front of a princess.

Fiona：   Thanks.

Donkey:	She's as nasty as you are.
Shrek:	You know, you're not exactly what I expected.
Fiona:	Well, maybe you shouldn't judge people before you get to know them.
Fiona:	Oh! Shall we?
Shrek:	Hold the phone! Oh, whoa, whoa, whoa, hold on now, where did that come from?
Fiona:	What?
Shrek:	That! Back there. That was amazing! Where did you learn that?
Fiona:	Well, when one lives alone, uh, one has to learn these things in case there's an... there's an arrow in your butt!
Shrek:	What? Oh, would you look at that?
Fiona:	Oh, no. This... this is all my fault. I'm so sorry.
Donkey:	Why? What's wrong?
Fiona:	Shrek's hurt.
Donkey:	Shrek's hurt. Shrek's hurt? Oh, no, Shrek's gonna die.
Shrek:	Donkey, I'm okay.
Donkey:	You can't do this to me, because I'm too young for you to die. Keep your legs elevated. Turn your head and cough. Does anyone know the Heimlich?
Fiona:	Donkey! Calm down. If you want to help Shrek, run into the woods and find me a blue flower with red thorns.
Donkey:	Blue flower, red thorns. Okay, I'm on it. Blue flower, red thorns. Blue flower, red thorns. Don't die, Shrek. If you see a long tunnel, stay away from the light!
Fiona&Shrek:	Donkey!
Donkey:	Oh, yeah. Right. Blue flower, red thorns. Blue flower, red thorns.
Shrek:	What are the flowers for?

Fiona:	For getting rid of Donkey.
Shrek:	Ah.
Fiona:	Now you hold still, and I'll yank this thing out.
Shrek:	Ow! Hey! Easy with the yankin'.
Fiona:	I'm sorry, but... but it has to come out.
Shrek:	No, it's tender.
Fiona:	Now, hold on.
Shrek:	What you're doing is the opposite of help.
Fiona:	Don't move.
Shrek:	Look, look, time out.
Fiona:	Would you... Okay. What do you propose we do?
Donkey:	Blue flower, red thorns. Blue flower, red thorns. Blue flower, red thorns. This would be so much easier if I wasn't color-blind! Blue flower, red thorns. Blue flower, red thorns.
Shrek:	Ow!
Donkey:	Hold on, Shrek! I'm comin'!
Shrek:	Ow! Not good.
Fiona:	Okay. Okay, I can nearly see the head. It's just about...
Shrek:	Ow! Ohh!
Donkey:	Ahem.
Shrek:	Nothing happened. We were just...
Donkey:	Look, if you wanted to be alone, all you had to do was ask. Okay?
Shrek:	Oh, come on! That's the last thing on my mind. The princess here was just... Ugh! Ow!
Donkey:	Hey, what's that? That's... Is that blood?

New Words

compliment [ˈkɒmplimənt]   *n.* a remark （or act） expressing praise and admiration 称赞；恭维

behave [biˈheiv]   *v.* conduct in a certain manner 举止端正

elevate [ˈeliveit]   *v.* raise from a lower to a higher position 举起；提拔

thorn [θɔːn]   *n.* a small sharp-pointed tip resembling a spike on a stem or leaf 刺；荆棘

yank [jæŋk]   *v.* pull, or move with a sudden movement 猛拉；猛拔

tender [ˈtendə]   *adj.* loving；gentle 亲切的；温和的

color-blind [ˈkʌləblaind]   *adj.* unable to distinguish colors 色盲的

Phrases and Expressions

kind of：sort of 有点儿；有几分

get rid of：go away from 赶走；剔除

make it up：step into peace 和解

eat up：eat all what is eaten 吃光；吃完

in case：in the event of 万一

calm down：make sb. become quiet and relax 使某人平静下来

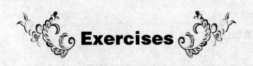

Exercises

① Comprehension of the Scene

Watch the scene carefully and tell if the following statements are TRUE or FALSE.

1. The story happens in the evening.

2. They had a great day yesterday.

3. Fiona is not like what Shrek expected before.

4. Shrek got injured.

5. Fiona yanked out the arrow from Shrek's butt.

② Vocabulary

Fill in the blanks with the words or phrases given below and change the form when necessary.

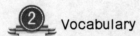

opposite	judge	behave	tender
yank	compliment	elevate	calm down

1. Your presence is a great _____.

2. _____ yourself; don't make a fool of yourself.

3. I _____ him to be about 40.

4. Reading good books _____ your mind.

5. He _____ out a loose tooth.

6. Don't mention his divorce; it's a very _____ subject.

7. Black and white are _____.

8. Experts say separation can help a couple on the way of divorce _____.

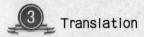 Translation

Translate the following sentences into English and use the words and expressions given in the brackets.

1. 她对他的过去有点好奇。(kind of)

2. 你想把他们赶走吗？(get rid of)

3. 我们把剩饭都吃光了。(eat up)

4. 她的家人很担心她在国外的生活。(worry about)

5. 这里什么事都没有发生。(happen)

Scene 4

The true form of Princess Fiona is revealed.

Donkey： What did you do with the princess?

Fiona： Donkey, I'm the princess.

Donkey： Aah!

Fiona： It's me, in this body.

Donkey： Oh, my God! You ate the princess! Can you hear me?

Fiona： Donkey!

Donkey： Listen, keep breathing!

Fiona： No!

Donkey： I'll get you out of there! Shrek! Shrek! Shrek!

Fiona： Shh.

Donkey： Shrek!

Fiona： This is me.

Donkey： Princess? What happened to you? You're, uh, uh, uh, different.

Fiona： I'm ugly, okay?

Donkey： Well, yeah! Was it something you ate? 'Cause I told Shrek those rats was a bad idea. You are what you eat, I said.

Fiona： No. I— I've been this way as long as I can remember.

Donkey: What do you mean? Look, I ain't never seen you like this before.

Fiona: It only happens when the sun goes down. "By night one way, by day another." This shall be the norm... "until you find true love's first kiss... and then take love's true form."

Donkey: Ah, that's beautiful. I didn't know you wrote poetry.

Fiona: It's a spell. When I was a little girl, a witch cast a spell on me. Every night I become this. This horrible, ugly beast! I was placed in a tower to await the day my true love would rescue me. That's why I have to marry Lord Farquaad tomorrow before the sun sets and he sees me... like this.

Donkey: All right, all right. Calm down. Look, it's not that bad. You're not that ugly. Well, I ain't gonna lie. You are ugly. But you only look like this at night. Shrek's ugly 24—7.

Fiona: But, Donkey, I'm a princess, and this is not how a princess is meant to look.

Donkey: Princess, how about if you don't marry Farquaad?

Fiona: I have to. Only my true love's kiss can break the spell.

Donkey: But, you know, um, you're kind of an ogre, and Shrek... well, you got a lot in common.

Fiona: Shrek?

Shrek: Princess, I... Uh, how's it going, first of all? Good? Um, good for me too. I'm okay. I saw this flower and thought of you, because it's pretty and... well, I don't really like it, but I thought you might like it 'cause you're pretty. But I like you anyway. I'd... uh, uh, I'm in trouble. Okay, here we go.

Fiona: I can't just marry whoever I want. Take a good look at me, Donkey. I mean, really, who could ever love a beast so hideous and ugly? "Princess" and "ugly" don't go together. That's why I can't stay here with Shrek. My only chance to live happily ever after is to marry my true love. Don't you see, Donkey? That's just how it has to be. It's the only way to break the spell.

New Words

breathe ［briːð］   *v.* take air into the lungs and send it out again 呼吸

norm ［nɔːm］   *n.* a standard or a pattern that is typical (of a group) 标准

poetry ［ˈpəuitri］   *n.* poems collectively or in general 诗的总称

spell ［spel］   *n.* words used as a charm supposed to have magic power 咒语

hideous ［ˈhidiəs］   *adj.* ①filling the mind with horror; frightful 可怕的；骇人听闻的 ②very ugly 丑恶的

Phrases and Expressions

do with：deal with 处理；对待

cast a spell：put magical force on 施咒语

calm down：become quiet or calm 冷静

in common：shared with one or more others 共同的

go together：①combine well with sth.；harmonize with sth. 与某事物配合良好；与某事物协调 ②exist at the same time or in the same place 同时或同地存在

break the spell：get rid of magical force 破除魔力

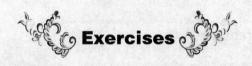

Exercises

 Comprehension of the Scene

Watch the scene carefully and write T（true）or F（false）for the following statements.

1. Fiona became ogress, because she ate those rats.

2. When Fiona was a little girl, a witch cast a spell on her.

3. Fiona was placed in a tower to await the day Shrek would rescue her.

4. Only Fiona's true love kiss can break the spell.

5. Shrek picked up a pretty flower and sent it to Fiona.

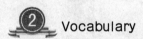 Vocabulary

Fill in the blanks with the words or phrases given below, and change the form when necessary.

breathe	norm	poetry	horrible	beast
in common	go together	do with	as long as	

1. A _____ monster attacked the helpless villagers.

2. Fish cannot _____ out of water.

3. We are having _____ weather. It is raining heavily all the day.

4. The lion is called the king of _____ .

5. His _____ was published last year.

6. _____ you drive carefully, you will be very safe.

7. Love and reason do not _____ .

8. The two sisters have nothing _____ .

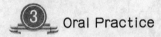 Oral Practice

The following are some useful phrases and expressions from the dialogue. Try to make a complete sentence with them.

1. Only _____ can break the spell.

2. _____ as long as _____.

3. It only happens when _____ .

4. _____ do not go together.

5. My only chance to _____ is to _____.

Scene 5

Shrek and Donkey return to the castle to stop the wedding, and Fiona soon finds her true love.

Shrek： I object!

Fiona： Shrek?

Farquaad： Oh, now what does he want?

Shrek： Hi, everyone. Havin' a good time, are ya? I love DuLoc, first of all. Very clean.

Fiona： What are you doing here?

Farquaad： Really, it's rude enough being alive when no one wants you, but showing up uninvited to a wedding...

Shrek： Fiona! I need to talk to you.

Fiona： Oh, now you wanna talk? Well it's a little late for that, so if you'll excuse me.

Shrek： But you can't marry him.

Fiona： And why not?

Shrek： Because... because he's just marrying you so he can be king.

Farquaad： Outrageous! Fiona, don't listen to him.

Shrek： He's not your true love.

Fiona： And what do you know about true love?

Shrek:	Well, I... Uh... I mean...
Farquaad:	Oh, this is precious. The ogre has fallen in love with the princess! Oh, good Lord. An ogre and a princess!
Fiona:	Shrek, is this true?
Farquaad:	Who cares? It's preposterous! Fiona, my love, we're but a kiss away from our "happily ever after". Now kiss me! Mmmm!
Fiona:	"By night one way, by day another." I wanted to show you before.
Shrek:	Well, uh, that explains a lot.
Farquaad:	Ugh! It's disgusting! Guards! Guards! I order you to get that out of my sight now! Get them! Get them both!
Fiona:	No, no!
Farquaad:	This hocus-pocus alters nothing. This marriage is binding and that makes me king! See? See?
Fiona:	No, let go of me! Shrek! No!
Farquaad:	Don't just stand there, you morons. Get out of my way!
Shrek:	Fiona! Arrgh!
Farquaad:	I'll make you regret the day we met. I'll see you drawn and quartered! You'll beg for death to save you!
Fiona:	No, Shrek.
Farquaad:	And as for you, my wife, Fiona! I'll have you locked back in that tower for the rest of your days. I am king! I will have order! I will have perfection! I will have... Aaah!
Donkey:	All right. Nobody move. I got a dragon here, and I'm not afraid to use it. I'm a donkey on the edge! Celebrity marriages. They never last, do they? Go ahead, Shrek.
Shrek:	Uh, Fiona?
Fiona:	Yes, Shrek?
Shrek:	I... I love you.
Fiona:	Really?

Shrek： Really, really.

Fiona： I love you too.

New Words

alive [ə'laiv]
adj. having life; living 有生命的；活着的

wedding ['wediŋ]
n. the ceremony or celebration of a marriage 婚礼

outrageous [aut'reidʒəs]
adj. ①grossly offensive to decency or morality 蛮横的 ②being well beyond the bounds of good taste 非常不文雅的

preposterous [pri'pɔstərəs]
adj. contrary to nature, reason, or common sense; absurd 荒谬的

hocus-pocus ['həukəs-'pəukəs]
n. ①foolishness or empty pretense used especially to disguise deception or chicanery 故弄玄虚的言词 ②trick performed by a magician or juggler; sleight-of-hand 魔术师或变戏法的人用的戏法；花招

alter ['ɔ:ltə]
v. change or make different; modify 变更、更改；修饰

binding [baindiŋ]
adj. imposing or commanding adherence to a commitment 有约束力的

moron ['mɔ:rən]
n. a person regarded as very stupid 白痴

regret [ri'gret]　　　　　　　　*v.* feel sorry, disappointed, or distressed about 后悔；惋惜

perfection [pə'fekʃən]　　　　*n.* ①the act or process of perfecting 完成的行为或过程②a person or a thing considered to be perfect 被认为完美的人或事③the state of being without a flaw or defect 完美

celebrity [si'lebrəti]　　　　　*n.* a famous person 名人

Phrases and Expression

out of one's sight：no longer visible 看不见

let go of：release as from one's grip 释放；放开

on the edge：①in a state of keen excitement, as from danger or risk 激动；兴奋 ②in a precarious position 边界状态

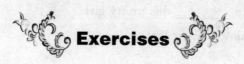

Exercises

 Comprehension of the Scene

Watch the scene carefully and write T（true）or F（false）for the following statements.

1. Shrek comes to stop Fiona's wedding.

2. Farquaad marries Fiona so he can be king.

3. Fiona has fallen in love with Farquaad.

4. Farquaad will have Shrek locked back in that tower for the rest of his days.

5. Shrek and Fiona fall in love with each other finally.

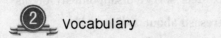

2 Vocabulary

Fill in the blanks with the words or phrases given below, and change the form when necessary.

disgusting	wedding	precious	regret	object	rude
alive	celebrity	out of my sight		fall in love with	

1. It's very _____ of her to leave without telling us.

2. I _____ that he was too young for the job.

3. We decided to delay our _____ until next year.

4. You should make good use of every _____ minute to study.

5. We _____ that we are unable to reconsider your case.

6. She became a _____ overnight.

7. He cannot help _____ this pretty girl.

8. I stood there until the car was _____ .

3 Oral Practice

The following are some useful phrases and expressions from the dialogue. Try to make a complete sentence with them.

1. It is rude enough _____ .

2. I will make you _____ .

3. _____ is disgusting.

4. First of all, _____ .

5. _____ has fallen in love with _____ .

Reading

Voicing Shrek

Large scale animated productions, like Shrek, depend on Hollywood celebrities to bring animated character voices to life. While having celebrities attached to an animated film is a major blow to voice actors, it provides major marketing potential for studios.

Celebrities starring in DreamWorks' Shrek include Mike Myers as Shrek, Eddie Murphy as Donkey, Cameron Diaz as Princess Fiona, and John Lithgow as Lord Farquaad.

The main star, of course, is Shrek—a disgusting ogre who reacts to his swamp home being invaded by fairy tale characters. As the star, it was important for the voice artist to bring out the disgusting habits of Shrek while still making him lovable.

"Shrek is no dreamboat, but Mike understood the heart and soul of the character and brought out his wonderful lovable qualities," says DreamWorks principle Jeffrey Katzenberg. In the way he brought Shrek's words to life, Mike gave him his heart and we were able to mold our physical character around his voice.

Sometimes voicing a character creates opportunities to improvise, which brings more life to the character.

Playing Shrek's "sidekick" is a donkey named Donkey. For the voice, the Shrek team selected Eddie Murphy. Murphy's last experience as a voice over artist came in Disney's Mulan where he played Mulan's sidekick, Mushu the Dragon.

Murphy freely admits that there are big differences between voice acting and live action acting.

"Animation is a much more collaborative process than acting with my body and my face," says Murphy. "It's a trip to have the director ask for a small inflection in your voice, and then, when the scene is drawn, you see how that slight change brings out the emotion. Another reason I like doing animated films is that, when they're done right, they're timeless, and my kids really get into them... They love hearing their father's voice come out of a cartoon."

Playing the role of the princess—who is unlike any past animated fairy tale princess—is actress Cameron Diaz. She describes the princess as "a little spark plug". What makes Shrek different for Diaz is that it is her first ever voicing of an animated character. She had no idea of what to expect.

When storyboard artists and other crew pitch an idea to the directors, they act out the characters in the sequence, including character dialogue. The Shrek filmmakers were so impressed with some of these performances that they cast some of their crew as animated character voices. This includes story artist Conrad Vernon as the Gingerbread Man, Chris Miller as Geppetto (and as the Magic Mirror), Cody Cameron as Pinocchio (and one of the three little pigs), and Christopher Knights as one of the three blind mice.

New Words

scale [skeil]

n. relation between the actual size of sth. and the map, diagram, etc. which represents it 比例；比率

potential [pə'tenʃ(ə)l]

adj. in existence and capable of being developed or used 潜在的；有潜力的

star [stɑː]	*v.* feature sb. 由某人主演
mold [məuld]	*v.* guide or control the development of sb. /sth. ; shape or influence sb. /sth. 指导或控制某人/某事物的发展；塑造或影响某人/某事物
improvise ['imprəvaiz]	*v.* compose or play (music), speak or act without previous preparation (即兴地或即席地) 创作、演奏、讲话、表演等
sidekick ['said,kik]	*n.* an assistant or close companion 助手；亲密伙伴
inflection [in'flekʃən]	*n.* a rise and fall of the voice in speaking (说话声音的) 抑扬变化
sequence ['siːkwəns]	*n.* a part of a cinema film dealing with one scene or topic (影片中描述一个场景或主题的) 连续镜头
process [prə'ses]	*n.* series of actions or operations performed in order to do, make or achieve sth. 步骤；程序；过程

Phrases and Expressions

impress sb. with sth.：have a favourable effect on sb. 给予某人深刻印象

Reading Comprehension

Read this article carefully and answer the following questions.

1. What do large scale animated productions depend on?

2. Can you name the celebrities starring in Shrek?

3. How did Mike Myers bring Shrek's words to life?

4. Why does Eddie Murphy like doing animated films?

5. What does Cameron Diaz describe the princess as and what does Shrek make it different for her?

6. What do you think of having celebrities attached to an animated film?

Chapter Two

Good Will Hunting

It's not your fault.

Main Characters

Will Hunting.....................................Matt Damon
Sean Maguire....................................Robin Williams
Skylar..Minnie Driver
Chuck...Ben Affleck

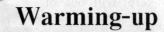

Warming-up

Synopsis

Will Hunting is a 20 years old Boston janitor who works cleaning classrooms at the Massachusetts Institute of Technology, one of the best and most famous universities in the world. He is an orphan who grew up in various foster homes, where he had been physically abused as a child. He is also an extraordinary mathematical genius with a photographic memory, who likes to solve math problems that an MIT pro-

fessor writes on a hallway chalkboard. For the students, these problems are too difficult to solve, but for Will, they're easy! One day, Professor Lambeau sees Will writing the answer to a problem on the chalkboard, but Will runs away before they can talk. Lambeau soon discovers many disturbing things about Will, including the fact that he is stuck in jail for having just physically attacked someone who had beaten him up many years earlier. Lambeau arranges with a judge to keep Will out of jail, as long as Will agrees to work on mathematical problems and to get psychological help. Will agrees to these conditions.

Will is too difficult a patient for the various psychologists that Lambeau asks to help, but eventually Lambeau goes to his old friend Sean Maguire, who is teach-

ing psychology at a local community college. Sean has many of his own problems to face, including the fact that his wife of 17 years had recently died from cancer. Still, he agrees to work with Will, and while the relationship is extremely difficult and emotionally explosive, Sean sticks with it because he is convinced he can help Will find some stability and happiness.

Over the next few months, Will becomes romantically involved with Skylar, a British student at Harvard University who has decided to go Medical School at Stanford University in California. Skylar falls in love with Will, and wants him to go with her to California, but Will is probably too scared to become so emotionally close to another person, or too scared to even leave Boston.

In the end, Lambeau simply wants Will to get a job where he would use his amazing mathematical intelligence, and even Chuck wants Will to find a life for himself that is far from the difficult working class lives that they both have now. Ultimately though, it is Sean who patiently gives Will the courage and direction he really needs to move on with his life.

New Words

janitor ['dʒænitə]	*n.* a caretaker 看门人
orphan ['ɔ:fən]	*n.* a person（esp. a child）whose parents are dead 父母双亡的人（尤指儿童）；孤儿
genius ['dʒi:njəs]	*n.* ①a person who has this ability 天才②exceptionally great mental or creative ability 天才；创造力
hallway ['hɔ:lwei]	*n.* corridor 走廊
psychological [saikə'lɔdʒikəl]	*adj.* ① of or affecting the mind 心理上的；精神上的②of or relating to psychology 心理学的；关于心理学的
psychologist [sai'kɔlədʒist]	*n.* a student of or an expert in psychology 心理学研究者；心理学家
explosive [iks'pləusiv]	*n.* a substance that is likely or able to explode 爆炸物；炸药
convince [kən'vins]	*v.* ①make sb. feel certain; cause sb. to realize 使某人确信；使某人明白②persuade 说服
stability [stə'biliti]	*n.* quality or state of being stable 稳定状态；沉稳
ultimately ['ʌltimətli]	*adv.* ①in the end; finally 最后；终于②at the most basic level; fundamentally 根本；基本上

Read the synopsis carefully and answer the following questions.

1. What happened to Will Hunting when he was a child?

2. Why is Will stuck in jail?

3. What is the agreement between Lambeau and Will?

4. Who is Sean Maguire?

5. Will doesn't want to go to California with Skylar，why?

Scene Study

Scene 1

Will and his friends entered the Harvard Bar and Chuck tried to talk with some girls in the bar.

Chuck:	Oh, hello.
Skylar:	Oh, hello.
Chuck:	Hi. How are ya?
Skylar:	Fine.
Chuck:	So, do you ladies, uh—
Skylar:	Come here often? Do I come here? I come here a bit. I'm here, you know, from time to time.
Chuck:	Do you go to school here?
Girl:	Yep.
Chuck:	Yeah, that's it. I think I had a class with you.
Skylar:	Oh, yeah. What class?
Chuck:	History.
Skylar:	Maybe.
Chuck:	Yes, I think that's what it was. You don't necessarily... may not remember me. You know, I like it here. It doesn't mean 'cause I go here, I'm a genius. I am very smart.
Clark:	Hey.
Chuck:	Hey, how's it goin'? How are ya?
Clark:	Good. How ya doin'? What class did you say that was?
Chuck & Skylar:	History.
Clark:	Just history? It must have been a survey course then.

Chuck:	Yeah, it was. It was surveys.
Clark:	Right.
Chuck:	You should check it out. It's a good course. It'd be a good class.
Clark:	How'd you like that course?
Chuck:	You know, frankly, I found that class, you know, rather elementary.
Clark:	Elementary. You know, I don't doubt that it was.
Chuck:	Yeah.
Clark:	I, uh, I remember that class. It was, um, it was just between recess and lunch.
Skylar:	Clark, why don't you go away?
Clark:	Why don't you relax?
Skylar:	Why don't you go away?
Clark:	I'm just havin' fun with my new friend. That's all.
Chuck:	Are we gonna have a problem?
Clark:	No, no, no, no. There's no problem here. I was just hoping you might give me some insight into the evolution of the market economy in the southern colonies. My contention is that prior to the Revolutionary War, the economic modalities, especially in the southern colonies, could most aptly be characterized as agrarian precapitalist.
Chuck:	Let me tell you something.
Will:	Of course that's your contention. You're a first-year grad student. You just got finished readin' some Marxian historian, Pete Garrison, probably you're gonna be convinced of that till next month when you get to James Lemon. Then you're gonna be talkin' about how the economies of Virginia and Pennsylvania were entrepreneurial and capitalist way back in 1740. That's gonna last until next year. You're gonna be in here

regurgitatin' Gordon Wood, talkin' about, you know, the prerevolutionary utopia and the capital-forming effects of military mobilization.

Clark: Well, as a matter of fact, I won't, because Wood drastically underestimates the impact of social. . .

Will: Wood drastically underestimates the impact of social distinctions predicated upon wealth, especially inherited wealth. You got that from Vickers' Work in Essex County. Page 98, right? I read that too. Were you gonna plagiarize the whole thing for us? Do you have any thoughts of your own on this matter? Or is that your thing? You come into a bar. You read some obscure passage. Then pretend pawn it off as your own. As your own idea just to impress some girls? Embarrass my friend? See, the sad thing about a guy like you is, in 50 years, you're gonna start doin' some thinkin' on your own. You're gonna come up with the fact that there are two certainties in life. One: Don't do that. And two: You dropped 150 grand on a fuckin' education you could' ve got for \$1. 50 in late charges at the public library.

Clark: Yeah, but I will have a degree, and you'll be servin' my kids fries at a drive through on our way to a skiing trip.

Will: Maybe, but at least I won't be unoriginal. If you have a problem with that, we could step outside. We could figure it out.

Clark: No, man, there's no problem. It's cool.

Will: It's cool?

Clark: Yeah.

Will: Cool.

Chuck: Damn right, it's cool. How do you like me now?

Will: Hi.

Skylar:	You're an idiot.
Will:	What?
Skylar:	You're an idiot. I've been sitting over there for 45 minutes... waiting for you to come and talk to me. But I'm tired now, and I have to go home. I couldn't sit there any more waiting for you.
Will:	I'm Will.
Skylar:	Skylar.
Will:	Skylar.
Skylar:	Oh, and by the way, that guy over there, Michael Bolton clone. He wasn't sitting with us, so to speak.
Will:	I know. I kinda got that impression.
Skylar:	Good. Okay. Well, I've got to go. Gotta get up early and waste some more money on my overpriced education.
Will:	No, I didn't mean you.
Skylar:	That's all right. There's my number. Maybe we can go out for coffee sometime.
Will:	All right, yeah. Maybe we can just get together and eat a bunch of caramels.
Skylar:	What do you mean?
Will:	When you think about it, it's as arbitrary as drinkin' coffee.
Skylar:	Oh. Yeah. Okay. Uh, right, then.
Girl:	Oh, come on. You're kidding.
Morgan:	Yo! There goes them fuckin' barneys right now with his skiin' trip.
Will:	Hold on.
Morgan:	We should've beat that old bitch's ass.
Will:	Do you like apples?
Clark:	Yeah.
Will:	Yeah? Well, I got her number! How do you like them apples?

New Words

survey [səˈvei] *v.* look carefully at sth. or sb. 仔细全面地观察

frankly [ˈfræŋkli] *adv.* ①in a frank manner 坦率地；坦白地 ②speaking honestly; to be truthful 说实话；诚实地

elementary [eliˈmentəri] *adj.* ①of or in the beginning stages (of a course of study)（一门课程的）入门阶段的 ② easy to solve or answer 容易解决的

recess [riˈses] *n.* ① a break between classes at school 学校的课间休息②a period of time when work or business is stopped，esp. in Parliament, the lawcourts，etc. 工作或业务活动的中止或暂停期间，尤指国会、法庭等的休会期、休庭期

evolution [i:vəˈlu:ʃən] *n.* (a theory of the) gradual development of the characteristics of plants and animals over many generations，esp. the development of more complicated forms from earlier，simpler forms 进化；进化论

colony [ˈkɔləni] *n.* a country or an area settled or conquered by people from another country and controlled by that country 殖民地

modality [məuˈdæliti]	*n.* a classification of propositions on the basis of whether they claim necessity or possibility or impossibility 样式；形式；形态
contention [kənˈtenʃən]	*n.* an assertion made in an argument 辩论时提出的论点
entrepreneurial [ɔntrəprəˈnjuːriəl]	*adj.* willing to take risks in order to make a profit 具有冒险、开拓精神的
capitalist [ˈkæpitəlist]	*adj.* based on or supporting capitalism 资本主义的 *n.* a person who owns or controls much capital 资本家；富人
utopia [juːˈtəupjə]	*n.* an imaginary place or state of things in which everything is perfect 乌托邦
inherited [inˈheritid]	*adj.* tending to occur among members of a family usually by heredity 通过继承得到的
plagiarize [ˈpleidʒiəraiz]	*v.* take (sb. else's ideas, words, etc) and use them as if they were one's own 剽窃、抄袭（他人的意念、言词等）
obscure [əbˈskjuə]	*adj.* ①not easily or clearly seen or understood; indistinct; hidden 不易看清的；不分明的；隐藏的 ②not well-known 不著名的

certainty ['sə:tənti]   *n.* a thing that is certain 确定的事
情

unoriginal ['ʌnə'ridʒənəl]   *adj.* not original; not being or pro-
ductive of sth. fresh and unusual 非
独创的；无创造性的

caramel ['kærəmel]   *n.* burnt sugar used for colouring
and flavouring food（食物着色或调
味用的）焦糖

arbitrary ['ɑːbiˌtrəri]   *adj.* based on personal opinion or
impulse，not on reason 任意的；任
性的；主观的

ass [æs]   *n.* ① the fleshy part of the human
body that you sit on 屁股、臀部② a
stupid person 傻瓜；笨蛋

Phrases and Expressions

prior to：before 在······之前

pawn sth. off as：sell sth. cheaply 把某物抵押掉

figure out：find the solution to（a problem or question）or understand the
meaning of 算出

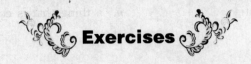

Exercises

 Comprehension of the Scene

Watch the scene carefully and answer the following questions.

1. Which class does Chuck tell the two girls he was in?

2. Those ideas that Clark said are his own opinions, aren't they?

3. According to Will, why does Clark pawn the passage off as his own ideas?

4. Why does Skylar say that Will was an idiot?

5. How does Will get Skylar's telephone number?

 Vocabulary and Structure

Fill in the blanks with the words given below, and change the form when necessary.

recess	embarrass	colony	obscure
elementary	entrepreneurial	arbitrary	plagiarize

1. This _____ school is affiliated to a university.

2. The committee is going into _____ for a couple of weeks.

3. This country used to be a British _____ in Asia.

4. Supply-side economics is supposed to promote savings, investment, and _____ creativity.

5. He has _____ most of the book from earlier study of the period.

6. The poem is _____ to those unlearned in the classics.

7. She dragged up that incident just to _____ me.

8. The choice of players for the team seems completely _____ .

 Translation

Translate the following sentences into English and use the words or expressions given in the brackets.

1. 这发生在我到达之前。(prior to)

2. 我琢磨不透他为什么要辞掉工作。(figure out)

3. 坦白讲，他没有你想象中的坏。(frankly)

4. 我们没有成功的把握。(certainty)

5. 气温已大大下降。(drastically)

Scene 2

Will refuses to cooperate with his therapist, so Gerry wants his roommate in college, Sean, to help.

Sean: Trust. Very important in a relationship. It's also very important in a clinical situation. Why is trust the most important thing in making a breakthrough with a client? Maureen, stop the oral fixation for a moment and join us. Vinnie.

Vinnie: Um... because, uh..., trust is, uh..., trust is life.

Sean: Wow. That's very deep. Thank you, Vinnie. Next time, get the notes from your brother. If a patient doesn't feel safe enough to trust you, then they won't be honest with you. Then there's really no point for them being in therapy. I mean, hey, if they don't trust you, you're never gonna get them to sleep with you. That should be the goal of any good therapist. Nail 'em while they're vulnerable. That's my motto. Oh, good, everyone's back. Welcome back, everybody.

Gerry: Hello, Sean.

Sean: Hey, Gerry. Um, ladies and gentlemen, we are in the presence of greatness. Professor Gerald Lambeau, Field's Medal winner for combinatorial mathematics.

Gerry: Hello.

Sean: Anyone knows what the Field's Medal is? It's a really big deal. It's like the Nobel Prize for math, except they only give it out once every four years. It's a great thing. It's an amazing honor. Okay, everybody, that's it for today. Thanks. We'll see you Monday. We'll be talking about Freud why he did enough cocaine to kill a small horse. Thank you.

Gerry: How are you?

Sean: It's good to see you.

Gerry: Good to see you. Sean, I think I got something interesting for ya.

Sean: Yeah? What, you have to have blood and urine? What's up?

Gerry: Why didn't you come to the reunion?

Sean: You know, I'm. . . I've been busy.

Gerry: You were missed.

Sean: Really?

Gerry: So how long has it been since we've seen each other?

Sean: Before Nancy died.

Gerry: Yeah, I'm sorry. I was in Paris. It was that damn conference. I got your card.

Sean: It was nice.

Will: Come here.

Chuck: Now that's a takedown. Hey, what happened? Did you get leniency or what?

Will: I got, uh, probation and then counseling two days a week.

Chuck: Joke. You're a smoothie. Come on, Morgan! Just submit!

Will: Hey, Bill, just. . . just get off him. We're gonna miss the game.

Sean: I've got a full schedule. I'm very busy.

Gerry: Sean, Sean. This. . . this boy is incredible. I've never seen anything like him.

Sean: What makes him so incredible, Gerry?

Gerry: You ever heard of Ramanujan?

Sean: Yeah, yeah. No.

Gerry: It's a man. He lived over 100 years ago. He was Indian. Dots, not feathers.

Sean: Not feathers. Yeah.

Gerry: He lived in this tiny hut somewhere in India. He had no formal education. He had no access to any scientific work.

Waiter: Coffee? You, sir?

Sean: Just a little.

Gerry: But he came across this old math book, and from the simple text, he was able to extrapolate theories that had baffled mathematicians for years.

Sean: Yes. Continued fractions. He wrote, uh—

Gerry: Well, he mailed it to Hardy at Cambridge.

Sean: Yeah, Cambridge. Yeah.

Gerry: And Hardy immediately recognized the brilliance of his work.

Sean: Mm-hmm.

Gerry: And brought him over to England, and then they worked together for years, creating some of the most exciting math theory ever done. This, this Ramanujan, his, his genius was unparalleled, Sean. Well, this boy's just like that.

Sean: Hmm.

Gerry: But he's, he's a bit defensive.

Sean: Hmm.

Gerry: I need someone who can get through to him.

Sean: Like me?

Gerry: Yeah, like you.

Sean: Why?

Gerry: Well, because you have the same kind of background.

Sean: What background?

Gerry: Well, you're from the same neighborhood.

Sean： He's from Southie?

Gerry： Yeah.

Sean： Boy genius from Southie. How many shrinks you go to before me?

Gerry： Five.

Sean： Let me guess. Barry?

Gerry： Yeah.

Sean： Henry?

Gerry： Yeah.

Sean： Not Rick?

Gerry： Sean, please, just meet with him once a week.

Sean： Mm-hmm.

Gerry： Please.

New Words

clinical ['klinikəl]

adj. of or relating to the examination and treatment of patients and their illnesses 临床的；有关临床的

oral ['ɔːrəl]

adj. ① not written; spoken 口头的；口述的 ② of, by or for the mouth 口的；用口的

therapy ['θerəpi]

n. any treatment designed to relieve or cure an illness or a disability 治疗；疗法

vulnerable ['vʌlnərəb(ə)l]

adj. exposed to danger or attack; unprotected 易受攻击的；无防御的

motto ['mɔtəu]

n. a short sentence or phrase chosen used as a guide or rule of behaviour 格言；座右铭

urine ['juərin]

n. waste liquid that collects in the bladder and is passed from the body 尿

conference ['kɔnfərəns]

n. a meeting for discussion or exchange of views 会议

leniency ['liːnjənsi]

n. mercifulness as a consequence of being tolerant 宽大；不严厉

probation [prə'beiʃən]

n. (a system of) keeping an official check on the behavior of (esp. young) people found guilty of crime as an alternative to send them to prison 缓刑（制）（尤指对年轻犯人施行的）

counseling ['kaunsəliŋ]

n. sth. that provides direction or advice as to a decision or a course of action 顾问服务

smoothie ['smuːði]

n. a person (usu. a man) who behaves in a smooth way 奉承而随和的人（通常指男子）

incredible [in'kredəbl]

adj. difficult to believe; amazing or fantastic 难以置信的；不可思议的；惊人的

extrapolate [eks'træpəleit]

v. ①calculate (an unknown quantity) approximately (from known values or measurements)（从已知的值或量）推算出（未知的量）② estimate（sth. unknown）from facts that are already known 由已知事实估计（未知事物）

baffle ['bæfl]   *v.* be too difficult for（sb.）to understand; puzzle 使（某人）困惑；难倒

unparalleled [ʌn'pærəleld]   *adj.* having no parallel or equal; unmatched 无比的；无双的

defensive [di'fensiv]   *adj.* ① showing anxiety to avoid criticism or attack; hiding faults 防备批评或攻击的；隐藏缺点的②used for or intended for defending 防御用的；防御性的

shrink [ʃriŋk]   *n.* psychiatrist 精神科医生
v. (cause sth. to) become smaller, esp. because of moisture or heat or cold（使某物）收缩，尤指因受潮、受热或受凉所致

Phrases and Expressions

access to：opportunity or right to use sth. or approach sb. 使用某物或接近某人的机会或权利
come across：find unexpectedly 偶然遇到；偶然发现

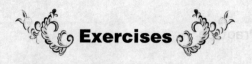 **Exercises**

 Comprehension of the Scene

Watch the scene carefully and answer the following questions.

1. What is the Field's Medal?

2. When did they meet each other last time?

3. Who is Ramanujan?

4. How did Gerry describe Will?

5. Does Sean agree to help Gerry?

 Vocabulary and Structure

Fill in the blanks with the words given below, and change the form when necessary.

baffle	therapy	submit	defensive
conference	shrink	oral	vulnerable

1. My _____ English is pretty rusty.

2. The _____ will be held in the Capitol in Washington.

3. We should _____ our plans to the council for approval.

4. The local or general use of low temperatures in medical _____ .

5. The potato is _____ to several pests.

6. The economy is _____ instead of growing.

7. When asked to explain her behavior, she gave a very _____ answer.

8. The question _____ me completely and I could not answer.

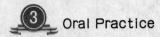 Oral Practice

What are true things about Gerry? Tick the right answers.

1. He is the Field's Medal winner for combinatorial mathematics.

2. He didn't come to the reunion.

3. He was in Paris when Nancy died.

4. He knew nothing about Nancy's death.

5. He thought that Will is a perfect guy.

6. He had found five therapists to help Will including Sean.

7. He thought that Will was just like Ramanujan.

8. He wanted Sean to meet Will once a month.

Scene 3

Will is having the therapy with Sean.

Will: Oh, you know, I read your book last night.

Sean: Oh, so you're the one.

Will: Do you still, uh...do you still counsel veterans?

Sean: No, I don't.

Will: Why not?

Sean: Well, I gave it up when my wife got sick.

Will: You ever wonder what your life would be like if you, uh, if you never met your wife?

Sean: What? Wonder if I'd be better off without her?

Will: No, no, no, I'm not saying, like, better off.

Sean: No.

Will: I didn't mean it like that.

Sean: It's all right. It's an important question, 'cause you'll have bad times, but that'll always wake you up to the good stuff you weren't paying attention to.

Will: And you don't regret meetin' your wife?

Sean: Why? 'Cause the pain I feel now? Oh, I got regrets, Will, but I don't regret a single day I spent with her.

Will: So when did you know, like, that she was the one for you?

Sean: October 21, 1975.

Will: Jesus Christ. You know the fuckin' day?

Sean: Oh, yeah, 'cause it was game six of the World Series, biggest game in Red Sox history.

Will: Yeah, sure.

Sean: My friends and I had slept out all night to get tickets.

Will: You got tickets?

Sean: Yep. Day of the game I was sittin' in a bar, waitin' for the game to start and in walks this girl. It was an amazing game though. You know, bottom of the eighth, Carbo ties it up. It was 6—6. It went to 12. Bottom of the 12th, in stepped Carlton Fisk, old Pudge. Steps up to the plate. You know, he's got that weird stance.

Will: Yeah, yeah.

Sean: And then— Boom! He clocks it, you know. High fly ball down the left field line! Thirty-five thousand people on their feet, yellin' at the ball. But that's nothin', 'cause Fisk, he's wavin' at the ball like a madman.

Will: Yeah, I've seen that.

Sean: Get over! Get over!

Will: Right.

Sean: Get over! Then it hits the foul pole. He goes ape-shit and 35, 000 fans. They charge the field, you know.

Will: Yeah, and he's fuckin' blowin' people outta the way.

Sean: Get outta the way! Get outta the way!

Will: I can't fuckin' believe you had tickets to that fuckin' game! Did you rush the field?

Sean: No, I didn't rush the fuckin' field. I wasn't there.

Will: What?

Sean: No, I was in a bar, havin' a drink with my future wife.

Will: You missed Pudge Fisk's home run to have a fuckin' drink with some lady you never met?

Sean: Yeah, but you should have seen her. She was a stunner.

Will: I don't care if...

Sean: Oh, no, no, she lit up the room.

Will: I don't care if Helen of Troy walks into the room.

Sean: Oh, Helen of Troy!

Will: That's game six! Oh, my God, and who were these friends of yours? They let you get away with that?

Sean: They had to.

Will: What did you say to 'em?

Sean: I just slid my ticket across the table. I said, "Sorry, guys. I gotta see about a girl."

Will: "I gotta go see about a girl?"

Sean: Yes!

Will: That's what you said? They let you get away with that?

Sean: Oh, yeah. They saw it in my eyes that I meant it.

Will: You're kiddin' me?

Sean: No, I'm not kidding you, Will. That's why I'm not talkin' right now about some girl I saw at a bar 20 years ago and how I always regretted not goin' over and talkin' to her. I don't regret the 18 years I was married to Nancy. I don't regret the six years I had to give up counseling when she got sick, and I don't regret the last years when she got really sick. And I sure as hell don't regret missin' a damn game. That's regret.

Will: Wow! Would have been nice to catch that game though.

Sean: I didn't know Pudge was gonna hit a home run.

New Words

veteran ['vetərən]　　　　　　*n.* a person with much or long experience, esp. as a soldier 经验丰富的人

weird [wiəd]　　　　　　　　*adj.* unconventional, unusual or bizarre 非传统的；不寻常的

stance [stæns]　　　　　　　*n.* moral or intellectual attitude (to sth.); standpoint（对某事物的）姿态、态度

stunner ['stʌnə]　　　　　　*n.* a person, esp. a woman, who is very attractive 极有魅力的人，尤指女子

slide [slaid]　　　　　　　　*v.* move smoothly along an even, polished or slippery surface 滑动

Phrases and Expressions

be better off: in a more fortunate or prosperous condition 情况更好
light up: make lighter or brighter 点亮；照亮

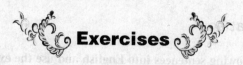 Exercises

 Comprehension of the Scene

Watch the scene carefully and answer the following questions.

1. When did Sean stop counseling veterans?

2. Did Sean think he would be better off if he never met his wife?

3. When did Sean know his wife was the one for him?

4. Why did Sean remember that date so clearly?

5. What did Sean say to his friends when he decided not to watch the game?

 Vocabulary and Structure

Fill in the blanks with the words given below, and change the form when necessary.

| veteran | hell | stuff | amazing |
| counsel | weird | slide | stance |

1. Good _____ has no price.

2. There has been some really good _____ on TV lately.

3. He looks like nothing on earth in those _____ clothes.

4. The book _____ off my knee.

5. His life has been _____ since his wife came back.

6. We listened to her _____ story with rapt attention.

7. What is your _____ on capital punishment?

8. His grandfather was a _____ of the World War Ⅱ.

 Translation

Translate the following sentences into English and use the expressions given in the brackets.

1. 灿烂的阳光照亮了他们的屋子。(light up)

2. 请注意这两个词之间的区别。(pay attention to)

3. 要是没有这家邻居，我们就过得更愉快了。(be better off)

4. 你应该戒烟，我去年就戒掉了。(give up)

Scene 4

After Skylar left, Will didn't go to the therapist's, instead of that, he came back to work.

Worker: Will, come on. Will! Will, that's it! We're done!

Gerry: I'm sitting in your office and the boy isn't here. Well, it's ten past 5: 00. An hour and ten minutes late. Well, if he doesn't show up and I file a report saying he wasn't here... and he goes back to jail, he won't be on my conscience. Okay. Fine.

Will: What's up?

Chuck: Thanks. Ah! God, that's good. So how's your lady?

Will: Ah, she's gone.

Chuck: Gone? Gone where?

Will: Med school. Medical school in California.

Chuck: Really?

Will: Yeah.

Chuck: When was this?

Will: It was, like, a week ago.

Chuck: That sucks. So, uh, when are you done with those meetings?

Will: I think the week after I'm 21.

Chuck: They are gonna hook ya up with a job or what?

Will: Yeah, fuckin' sit in a room and do long division for the next 50 years.

Chuck: Nah, probably make some nice bank though.

Will: I'm gonna be a fuckin' lab rat.

Chuck: Better than this shit. Way outta here.

Will: What do I want a way outta here for? I mean, I'm gonna fuckin' live here the rest of my life. You know, be neighbors. You know, have little kids. Fuckin' take 'em to Little League together up Foley Field.

Chuck: Look, you're my best friend, so don't take this the wrong way. But in 20 years if you're still livin' here, comin' over to my house to watch the Patriots games, still workin' construction, I'll fuckin' kill ya.

Will: What?

Chuck: That's not a threat. That's a fact. I'll fuckin' kill ya.

Will: What the fuck are you talkin' about?

Chuck: Look, you got something none of us have.

Will: Oh, come on! Why is it always this? I fuckin' owe it to myself to do this or that. What if I don't want to?

Chuck: No, no, no. Fuck you. You don't owe it to yourself. You owe it to me, 'cause tomorrow I'm gonna wake up and I'll be 50, and I'll still be doin' this shit. That's all right. That's fine. I mean, you're sittin' on a winnin' lottery ticket. You're too much of a pussy to cash it in, and that's bullshit. 'Cause I'd do fuckin' anything to have what you got. So would any of these fuckin' guys. Be an insult to us if you're still here in 20 years. Hangin' around here is a fuckin' waste of your time.

Will: You don't know that.

Chuck: I don't?

Will: No. You don't know that.

Chuck: Oh, I don't know that. Let me tell you what I do know. Every day I come by your house, and I pick you up. We go out and have a few drinks and few laughs, and it's great. You know what the best part of my day is? It's for about ten seconds: from when I pull up to the curb and when I get to your door. 'Cause I think maybe I'll get up there and I'll knock on the door and you won't be there. No "good-bye", no "see ya later". No nothing. You just left. I don't know much, but I know that.

New Words

file [fail]　　　　　　　*v.* send sth. so that it may be re-corded 送交某物以便备案

conscience ['kɔnʃəns]　　*n.* a person's awareness of right and wrong with regard to his own thoughts and actions 良心；是非感

suck [sʌk]　　　　　　*n.* bad things〈俚〉糟糕；太烂了
　　　　　　　　　　　　v. draw（liquid or air, etc.）into the mouth by using the lip muscles（用嘴）吸（液体或气体等）

hook [huk]　　　　　　*v.* （cause sth. to）be fastened with or as if with a hook or hooks 钩住（某物）

division [di'viʒən]　　　*n.* dividing one number by another 除；除法

threat [θret]　　　　　*n.* an expression of one's intention to punish or harm sb., esp. if he does not obey 恐吓；威胁

owe [əu]　　　　　　　*v.* be in debt to（sb.）（for goods, etc.）（因货物等）欠（某人）债

lottery ['lɔtəri]　　　　*n.* way of raising money by selling numbered tickets and giving prizes to the holders of numbers selected at random 抽彩给奖法

pussy ['pusi]　　　　　*n.* （used by and to young children）

cat（小儿语）猫咪

insult ['insʌlt]   *n.* remarks or actions that offend or hurt 侮辱；辱骂

curb [kə:b]   *n.* ①a strap or a chain passing under a horse's jaw, used to restrain the horse 马勒；马嚼子 ②a thing that restrains or controls 起约束或控制作用的事物

Phrases and Expressions

show up：appear or become visible 露出；露面

cash in：take advantage of or profit from sth. 从某事物中获得利益或利润

hang around：be standing about (a place) doing nothing definite; move away 无所事事地待在（某处）；荡来荡去

pull up：(cause a vehicle to) come to a halt （使车辆）停下

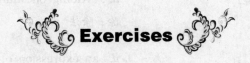

Exercises

 Comprehension of the Scene

Watch the scene carefully and answer the following questions.

1. When should Will be in Sean's office?

2. What will Gerry do if Will doesn't show up?

3. When did Skylar leave? Where did she go?

4. What is Will's plan for his future?

5. According to Chuck, when is the best part of his day?

Vocabulary and Structure

Fill in the blanks with the words given below, and change the form when necessary.

rat	owe	suck	conscience
lab	threat	lottery	insult

1. She had the prize-winning _____ ticket.

2. He was not in his office and I eventually tracked him down in the _____ .

3. Don't _____ your thumb; it's so dirty.

4. He _____ his success more to luck than to ability.

5. I'm sorry for what I said; I never meant to _____ you.

6. Some people think that machinery is a _____ to their jobs.

7. I got nothing to hide. My _____ is clear.

8. They said they'd help but they've _____ on us.

3 Translation

Translate the following sentences into English and use the expressions given in the brackets.

1. 我们的婚礼，乔治叔叔没有来，因为他忘了。(show up)

2. 如果你看到有人在这儿闲荡，就叫他们走开。(hang around)

3. 司机在大门前停下车子。(pull up)

4. 他把自己的成功归功于老师的鼓励和同学的帮助。(owe to)

5. 我仍然认为你误会了。(take it the wrong way)

Scene 5

As Will didn't show up, Gerry quarreled with Sean.

Gerry: This is a disaster, Sean. I brought you in here because I wanted you to help me with the boy, not to run him out.

Sean: I know what I'm doing with the boy.

Gerry: I don't care if you have a rapport with the boy! I don't care if you have a few laughs, even at my expense. But don't you dare undermine what I'm trying to do here.

Sean: Undermine?

Gerry: This boy is at a fragile point right now.

Sean: I do understand. He is at a fragile point. OK? He's got problems.

Gerry: What problems does he have, Sean? That he's better off as a janitor? That he's better off in jail? Better off hanging out with a bunch of retarded gorillas?

Sean: Why do you think he does that, Gerry? You have any fuckin' clue, why?

Gerry: He can handle the problems. He can handle the work. He obviously handled you.

Sean: Gerry, listen to me. Listen. Why is he hiding? Why doesn't he trust anybody? Because the first thing that happened to him, he was abandoned by the people who supposed to love him the most.

Gerry: Oh, come on. Don't give me that Freudian crap.

Sean: Why does he hang out with those retarded gorillas, as you call them? Because any one of them, if he asked them to, would take a bat to your head, OK? That's called loyalty.

Gerry: Yeah, that's very touching.

Sean: Who's he handling? He pushes people away before they have a chance to leave him. It's a defense mechanism, all right? For 20

years, he's been alone because of that. If you push him right
now, it's gonna be the same thing all over again. I'm not gonna
let that happen to him.

Gerry: Don't you do that, Sean.

Sean: What, Gerry?

Gerry: Don't do that. Don't infect him with the idea that it's okay to
quit, that it's okay to be a failure. Because it's not okay, Sean!
And if you're angry at me for being successful, for being what
you could have been. . . Sean.

Sean: I'm not angry at you.

Gerry: Oh, yes, you're angry at me, Sean. You resent me, but I'm not
gonna apologize for any, any success I've had. You're angry at
me for doing what you could have done! But ask yourself,
Sean. . . ask yourself if you want Will to feel that way. . . if you
want him to feel like a failure?

Sean: You arrogant shit! That's why I don't come to the goddamn reunions, 'cause I can't stand that look in your eye. You know?
That condescending, embarrassed look.

Gerry: Oh, come on, Sean.

Sean: You think I'm a failure. I know who I am. I'm proud of what I
do. It was a conscious choice. I didn't fuck up! And you and
your cronies think I'm some sort of pity case. You and your kiss-
ass chorus following you around going, "The Field's medal! The
Field's medal!" Why are you still so fuckin' afraid of failure?

Gerry: It's about my medal, isn't it? Oh, God, I could go home and get
it for you. You can have it.

Sean: Please don't. Shove the medal up your fuckin' ass, all right?
'Cause I don't give a shit about your medal, because I knew you
before you were a mathematical god, when you were pimple-
faced and homesick and didn't know what side of the bed to piss
on.

Gerry: Yeah, you were smarter than me then and you're smarter than me now. So don't blame me for how your life turned out. It's not my fault.

Sean: I don't blame you! It's not about you! You mathematical dick! It's about the boy! He's a good kid! And I won't see you fuck him up like you're tryin' to fuck up me right now. I won't see you make him feel like a failure too!

Gerry: He won't be a failure, Sean!

Sean: But if you push him, Gerry! If you ride him!

Gerry: I am what I am today because I was pushed and because I learned to push myself.

Sean: He's not you! You get that!

Will: I can come back.

Gerry: No, come in. Uh, I was just leaving.

Sean: A lot of that stuff goes back a long way between me and him. You know. Not about you.

Will: What is that?

Sean: This is your file. I have to send it back to the judge for evaluation.

Will: Oh. Hey, you're not gonna fail me, are you? What's it say?

Sean: Wanna read it?

Will: Why? Have you had any, uh, experience with that?

Sean: Twenty years of counseling. Yeah, I've seen some pretty awful shit.

Will: I mean, have you had any experience with that?

Sean: Personally? Yeah. Yeah, I have.

Will: It sure ain't good.

Sean: My father was an alcoholic. Mean fuckin' drunk. He'd come home hammered, lookin' to whale on somebody. So I'd provoke him so he wouldn't go after my mother and little brother. Interesting nights when he wore his rings.

Will: He used to just put a wrench, a stick and a belt on the table. Just say, "Choose".

Sean: Well, I am gotta go with the belt there.

Will: I used to go with the wrench.

Sean: Why the wrench?

Will: 'Cause fuck him, that's why.

Sean: Your foster father?

Will: Yeah. So, uh, what is it, like, Will has an attachment disorder? Is it all that stuff? Fear of abandonment? Is that why I broke up with Skylar?

Sean: I didn't know you had.

Will: Yeah, I did.

Sean: You wanna talk about it?

Will: No.

Sean: Hey, Will, I don't know a lot. You see this? All this shit? It's not your fault.

Will: Yeah, I know that.

Sean: Look at me, son. It's not your fault.

Will: I know.

Sean: No. It's not your fault.

Will: I know.

Sean: No, no, you don't. It's not your fault. Hmm?

Will: I know.

Sean: It's not your fault.

Will: All right.

Sean: It's not your fault. It's not your fault.

Will: Don't fuck with me.

Sean: It's not your fault.

Will: Don't fuck with me, all right? Don't fuck with me, Sean, not you.

Sean: It's not your fault. It's not your fault.

Will： My God! My God! I'm so sorry! My God!
Sean： Fuck'em, OK?

New Words

disaster [di'zɑːstə]　　　*n.* an event that causes great harm or damage, e. g. a fire, a serious defeat, the loss of a large sum of money 灾难；灾祸

rapport [ræ'pɔːt]　　　*n.* sympathetic and harmonious relationship 融洽和谐的关系

undermine [ˌʌndə'main]　*v.* weaken gradually or insidiously 逐渐削弱或暗中破坏

fragile ['frædʒail]　　　*adj.* easily damaged or broken; delicate 易受伤害的；易碎的

bunch [bʌntʃ]　　　*n.* a number of things (usu. of the same kind) growing, fastened or grouped together 串；束；卷

retarded [ri'tɑːdid]　　*adj.* backward in physical or (esp.) mental development 身体或（尤指）精神发育迟缓的

gorilla [gə'rilə]　　　*n.* a very large powerful African ape 大猩猩（产于非洲）

crap [kræp]　　　*n.* ①nonsense; rubbish 胡扯；废话 ②excrement 屎

loyalty ['lɔiəlti]　　　*n.* being true and faithful; loyal behaviour 忠诚；忠诚行为

infect [in'fekt]

v. ①fill sb.'s mind with undesirable ideas 用坏思想感染某人的思想 ②cause sb./sth. to have a disease; contaminate sb./sth. 使某人/某物传染、感染

resent [ri'zent]

v. feel bitter, indignant or angry about (sth. hurtful, insulting, etc.) （因受到伤害、侮辱等）对（某事物）感到愤恨、怨恨或气愤

arrogant ['ærəgənt]

adj. showing too much pride in oneself and too little consideration for others 傲慢的；自大的

condescending [kɔndi'sendiŋ]

adj. (used of behavior or attitude) characteristic of those who treat others as undignified or below one's level of importance 谦逊的；故意屈尊的

embarrassed [im'bærəst]

adj. feeling or caused to feel uneasy and self-conscious 尴尬的；局促不安的

crony ['krəuni]

n. close friend or companion 密友；亲密的伙伴

pimple ['pimpl]

n. small raised inflamed spot on the skin 小脓疱；粉刺

evaluation [i,vælju'eiʃən]

n. act of ascertaining or fixing the

value or worth of 估价；评价

alcoholic [ˌælkəˈhɔːlik]　　　　*n.* a person who drinks too much alcohol or suffers from alcoholism 酒鬼；酒精中毒的人

provoke [prəˈvəuk]　　　　*v.* make (sb.) angry 激怒（某人）

wrench [rentʃ]　　　　*n.* a hand tool that is used to hold or twist a nut or bolt 扳钳

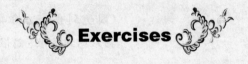

Exercises

 Comprehension of the Scene

Watch the scene carefully and answer the following questions.

1. According to Sean，why is Will hiding? Why doesn't he trust anybody?

2. Why has Will been alone for 20 years?

3. Why didn't Sean come to the reunions?

4. What will Sean do with Will's file?

5. What did Sean do when his drunk father came home?

 Vocabulary and Structure

Fill in the blanks with the words given below，and change the form when necessary.

| rapport | loyalty | arrogant | apologize |
| infect | resent | abandon | disaster |

1. After the _____ there were many who wanted food and shelter.

2. The actor developed a close _____ with his audience.

3. They had _____ all hope.

4. My judgment was frequently faulty, but my _____ to the nation could not be questioned.

5. The young teacher _____ the whole class with her enthusiasm.

6. I _____ having to get his permission for everything I do.

7. You must _____ to your sister for being so rude.

8. One should never be _____ even when he is at his best.

3 Further Study

Try to make a complete sentence with useful phrases and expressions from the dialogue.

1. I don't care if _____.

2. I want you to _____.

3. Ask yourself if you _____.

4. Don't blame me for _____.

5. Why do you think _____?

Reading

In essence, *Good Will Hunting* is an ordinary story told well. Taken as a whole, there's little that's special about this tale — it follows a traditional narrative path, leaves the audience with a warm, fuzzy feeling, and never really challenges or surprises us. But it's intelligently written (with dialogue that is occasionally brilliant), strongly directed, and nicely acted. So, while *Good Will Hunting* is far from a late-year masterpiece, it's a worthwhile sample of entertainment.

Like *Scent of a Woman*, which was released around this time of the season five years ago, *Good Will Hunting* is about the unlikely friendship that develops between a world-weary veteran and a cocky young man. The formula for the two films is similar — both of the principals learn from each other as they slowly break down their barriers on the way to a better understanding of life and their place in it — but the characters are different. Al Pacino's Slade was a larger-than-life individual; Robin Williams' Sean Mcguire is much more subtle. And Matt Damon's Will Hunting uses pugnaciousness to supplant the blandness of Chris O'donnell's Charlie.

Will is a troubled individual. As a child, he was the frequent victim of abuse. An orphan, he was in and out of foster homes on a regular basis. Now, not yet 21 years old, he has accumulated an impressive rap sheet. He has a short temper and any little incident can set him off like a spark in a tinder box. But he's a mathematical genius with a photographic memory and the ability to conceive simple solutions to complex problems. While working as a janitor at MIT, he delights in anonymously proving theorems on the math building's hall blackboards. Then, one evening, his anonymity is shattered when Professor Lambeau (Stellan Skarsgard) catches him at work. Will flees, but Lambeau tracks him down. Unfortunately, by the time the professor finds him, Will is in jail for assaulting a police offer.

The judge agrees to release Will under two conditions: that he spend one day a week meeting with Lambeau and that he spend one day a week meeting with a therapist. Eventually, once several psychologists have rejected the belligerent young man, Sean Mcguire, a teacher at Bunker Hill Community College, agrees to take the case. After a rocky start, the two form a rapport and Will begins to explore issues and emotions he had walled up behind impregnable armor. And, as Will advances his self-awareness in sessions with Sean, he also learns about friendship from his buddy, Chuck (Ben Affleck), and love from a Harvard co-ed named Skylar (Minnie Driver).

The script, by co-stars Matt Damon and Ben Affleck, is not a ground-breaking piece of literature, and occasionally resorts to shameless manipulation. The characters are well-developed, however, and there are times when the dialogue positively sparkles. At one point, Will comments that a session with Sean is turning into a "Taster's Choice Moment". Later, Will gives a brilliant, breathless diatribe against the NSA that has the rhythm of something written by Kevin Smith. (Note: Since Smith co-executive produced *Good Will Hunting*, it's not out of the question that he had some input into this scene.)

Director Gus Van Sant (*Drugstore Cowboy*, *To Die For*) culls genuine emotion from his actors, and this results in several affecting and powerful scenes. There's an edginess to some of the Sean/Will therapy sessions, and the offscreen chemistry between Matt Damon and Minnie Driver (who became romantically linked while making this film) translates effectively to the movie — the Will/Skylar relationship is electric. Likewise, the companionability of Damon and Affleck is apparent in the easygoing nature of Will and Chuck's friendship. Many of the individual scenes are strong enough to earn *Good Will Hunting* a recommendation, even if the overall story is somewhat generic.

Matt Damon, who recently starred as the idealistic young lawyer in

The Rainmaker, is solid (although not spectacular) as Will. Minnie Driver (last seen in *Grosse Pointe Blank*) adds another strong performance to a growing résumé (and it's refreshing that she was allowed to keep her British accent rather than having to attempt an American one). The outstanding performance of the film belongs to Robin Williams, whose Sean is sad and wise, funny and somber. Arguably the best dramatic work in the actor's career (alongside what he did in *The Fisher King*), Williams' portrayal could earn him a Best Supporting Actor Oscar nomination. Adequate support is provided by Ben Affleck (*Chasing Amy*) and Stellan Skarsgard (*Breaking the Waves*).

Like most of what comes before it, the ending of *Good Will Hunting* is completely predictable. But meeting expectations and following a familiar path aren't always bad things in a movie, provided the film accomplishes those goals with a modicum of style and an attention to detail. *Good Will Hunting* does both, and, as a result, earns a rating commensurate with the "good" in the title.

New Words

narrative ['nærətiv]	*adj.* of, or in the form of story-telling 叙述的；叙事体的
fuzzy ['fʌzi]	*adj.* having a soft and fluffy texture 绒毛般的；毛茸茸的
intelligent [in'telidʒənt]	*adj.* showing sound judgment and rationality 聪明的；有才智的
cocky ['kɔki]	*adj.* conceited; arrogant 自高自大的；趾高气扬的
barrier ['bæriə]	*n.* a thing that prevents or controls

progress or movement 阻碍进步或控制活动的事物

subtle ['sʌtl]　　　　　　*adj.* not easy to detect or describe; fine; delicate 难以察觉或描述的；细微的；精细的

pugnacious [pʌg'neiʃəs]　　*adj.* tough, callous 好斗的

supplant [sə'plɑːnt]　　　*v.* replace 取代

blandness ['blændnis]　　　*n.* the trait of exhibiting no personal embarrassment or concern 平淡

foster ['fɔstə]　　　　　　*v.* take care of and bring up (a child that is not legally one's own) 照顾、抚养（法律上不属于自己的孩子）

accumulate [ə'kjuːmjuleit]　*v.* gradually get or gather together an increasing number or quantity of (sth.); get (sth.) in this way 积累、聚积；聚集而成

tinder ['tində]　　　　　　*n.* any dry substance that catches fire easily 干燥易燃之物

anonymously [ə'nɔniməsli]　*adv.* without giving a name 用匿名的方式

theorem ['θiərəm]　　　　　*n.* rule in algebra, etc., esp. one expressed as a formula 代数等的定理

shatter ['ʃætə]　　　　　　*v.* break suddenly and violently into small pieces 突然而剧烈地裂成碎片；粉碎

assault [ə'sɔːlt]　　　　　　　*v.* make an assault on (sb.) 突袭；突击

belligerent [bi'lidʒərənt]　　*adj.* waging war; engaged in a conflict 交战的；卷入冲突的

impregnable [im'pregnəbl]　　*adj.* so strong and well-constructed that it cannot be entered or captured 坚固得不能进入或无法夺取的

manipulation [mə,nipju'leiʃən]　*n.* exerting shrewd or devious influence esp. for one's own advantage 操作；操纵；控制

cull [kʌl]　　　　　　　　　　*v.* kill (a certain number of usu. weaker animals) in a herd, in order to reduce its size 杀掉（通常为族群中一定数量的体弱多病者）以减少兽群总数

edginess ['edʒinis]　　　　　　*n.* feelings of anxiety that make you tense and irritable 急躁

generic [dʒi'nerik]　　　　　　*adj.* shared by or including a whole group or class; not specific 属的；类的；一般的

accent ['æksənt]　　　　　　　*n.* national, local or individual way of pronouncing words 民族、地方或个人的口音、腔调

portrayal [pɔː'treiəl]　　　　　*n.* a word picture of a person's appearance and character 画像；描述

predictable [pri'diktəb(ə)l]   *adj.* that can be foretold 可预言的；可预报的

modicum ['mɔdikəm]   *n.* small or moderate amount of sth. 少量；适量

commensurate [kə'menʃərit]   *adj.* in the right proportion to sth.; appropriate 与某事物成比例的；适当的

Phrases and Expressions

rap sheet: the daily written record of events (as arrests) in a police station 警察局档案

track down: pursue for food or sport (as of wild animals) 追踪；追捕

resort to: make use of sth. for help; adopt sth. as an expedient 诉诸；求助于

Reading Comprehension

Read this article carefully and answer the following questions.

1. Why is this tale special?
2. What is the difference between *Good Will Hunting* and *Scent of a Woman*?
3. Does Will have a happy childhood?
4. Try to describe the 21-year-old Will.
5. What is Will's strong point?
6. What are the two conditions that the judge agrees to release Will?
7. Finally, who agreed to take Will's case?
8. As the ending of *Good Will Hunting* is completely predictable, what makes this film successful?

Chapter Three

Little Miss Sunshine

Life is one fucking beauty contest after one another.

Main Characters

Olive Hoover.....................................Abigail Breslin
Richard Hoover...................................Greg Kinnear
Dwayne Hoover.....................................Paul Dano
Grandpa Edwin Hoover........................Alan Arkin
Sheryl Hoover....................................Toni Collette
Frank Ginsberg..................................Steve Carell

Warming-up

Synopsis

Sheryl Hoover (Toni Collette) is an overworked mother of two children, who lives in Albuquerque, New Mexico. Her brother, Frank (Steve Carell), is a scholar of French author Proust and a homosexual, temporarily living at home with the family after having attempted suicide. Sheryl's husband Richard (Greg Kinnear) is a Type A personality striving to build a career as a motivational speaker and life coach. Dwayne (Paul Dano), Sheryl's son from a previous marriage, is a Nietzsche-reading teenager who has taken a vow of silence until he can accomplish his dream of becoming a test pilot. Richard's foulmouthed fa-

ther, Edwin (Alan Arkin), recently evicted from a retirement home for snorting heroin, also lives with the family.

Olive, Sheryl's daughter, learns she has qualified for the "Little Miss

Sunshine" beauty pageant that is being held in Redondo Beach, California in two days. So the whole family goes on an 800-mile road trip to California in their yellow Volkswagen T2 Microbus. On the way to California, one

thing happens after another and the overall atmosphere in the family is changing gradually.

The climax takes place at the beauty pageant. In the hotel, the family sees Olive's competition: slim, hypersexualized pre-teen girls with teased hair and capped teeth. As Olive's turn to perform in the talent portion of the pageant draws near, Richard and Dwayne recognize that Olive is certain to be humiliated and wanting to spare her feelings. They run to the dressing room to talk her out of performing. Sheryl, however, insists that they "let Olive be Olive", and Olive goes on stage. Olive scandalizes and horrifies most of the audience and pageant judges with a burlesque performance that she joyfully performs while oblivious to their reactions.

The family is next seen outside the hotel's security office where they are given their freedom in return for a promise never to enter a beauty pageant in the state of California again. Piling into the van with the horn still honking, they happily smash through the barrier of the hotel's toll booth and head back to their home.

New Words

overworked [ˌəuvəˈwəːkt]   *adj.* work excessively hard 工作过度的

homosexual [ˌhəuməuˈseksjuəl]   *adj.* sexually attracted to members of one's own sex 同性恋的

temporarily ['tempərərili]

adv. for a limited time only; not permanently 暂时地；临时地

motivational [məuti'veiʃənəl]

adj. of or relating to motivation 激发性的

previous ['pri:vjəs]

adj. coming before in time or order（时间或顺序上）先的；前的

foulmouthed [faul 'mauθt]

adj. impolite; talking about sth. foul 出口粗俗的；出言不逊的

snort [sno:t]

v. ①sniff (drugs) 从鼻孔吸入（毒品）②force air out through the nostrils with a loud noise 喷鼻息作声；打响鼻

pageant ['pædʒənt]

n. spectacular display 选美比赛

climax ['klaimæks]

n. most interesting or significant event or point in time; culmination 顶点；极点；高潮

hypersexualized
[ˌhaipə'seksjuə'laizd]

adj. (sth.) reminds people of sex 勾起性欲的

capped [kæpt]

adj. used especially of front teeth having artificial crowns 给牙齿加上假牙冠

humiliate [hju(:)'milieit]

v. make (sb.) feel ashamed or disgraced; lower the dignity or self-respect of 使（某人）感到羞耻或不光彩；使丧失尊严或自尊

scandalize ['skændəlaiz]	*v.* shock; offend the moral feelings or the ideas of etiquette of 使某人愤慨或震惊
burlesque [bəːˈlesk]	*adj.* of, relating to or using a satirical imitation（滑稽或夸张性）模仿的
oblivious [əˈbliviəs]	*adj.* unaware of or not noticing sth.; having no memory of sth. 未觉察的；不注意的
horn [hɔːn]	*n.* device for sounding a warning signal 示警装置
honk [hɔŋk]	*v.* make a loud noise 发出汽车喇叭声

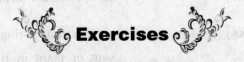

Read the synopsis carefully and answer the following questions.

1. Who is Frank? What does he do? Why does he come to live with the family?

2. Who is Dwayne? What is his vow about?

3. Who is Edwin? Why does he live with the family?

4. Why does the whole family go to California?

5. When does the climax take place?

6. What happens to Olive on the stage?

7. Does the movie end merrily?

Scene Study

Scene 1

The family is talking about Dwayne's vow of silence.

Frank: So, Sheryl, I couldn't help noticing Dwayne has stopped speaking.

Sheryl: Oh, yeah, he's taken a vow of silence.

Frank: You've taken a vow of silence?

Sheryl: Yeah. He's gonna join the Air Force Academy, become a test pilot and he's taken a vow of silence until he reaches that goal.

Frank: You're kidding?

Olive: Hi, Uncle Frank.

Frank: Oh, hey, Olive. Wow, you're gettin' big. Almost like a real person.

Olive: What happened to your arms?

Sheryl: Olive.

Frank: That's all right. I had a little accident. I'm okay.

Richard: How's the, uh, routine coming, honey?

Olive: It's good.

Richard: Yeah? When are you gonna show it to us?

Olive: I don't know. It's up to grandpa.

Grandpa: A couple of days. It still needs work. What's that? Chicken? Every night it's the fuckin' chicken! Holy God Almighty! It is possible just once. . .

Richard: Dad!

Grandpa: We could get something to eat around here, that's not the god damn fucking chicken?

Richard: Hey, Dad! Dad!

Grandpa: I'm just sayin' Christ.

Richard: When you want to start cooking your own food, you're more than welcome.

Grandpa: At Sunset Manor, you know...

Richard: If you like Sunset Manor, you shouldn't have got kicked out, right?

Grandpa: For God's sakes.

Frank: So when did you start with the vow?

Richard: It's been nine months, Frank. He hasn't said a word. Not one. I think it shows tremendous discipline.

Sheryl: Richard.

Richard: I really do. Really. I think we could learn something from Dwayne. Dwayne has a goal. He has a dream. It may not be my dream, may not be yours, but he's pursuing it with great conviction and focus. In fact, I was thinking about the nine steps.

Grandpa: Oh, for crying out loud!

Richard: And how Dwayne's utilizing seven of them in his personal quest to self-fulfillment.

Sheryl: Richard, please.

Richard: Well, I'm just saying I've come around. I think he could use our support.

New Words

vow [vaʊ] n. a solemn promise or undertaking, esp. of a religious nature 誓约；誓言（尤指宗教的）
v. swear, promise or declare solemnly 立誓；发誓

routine [ruː'tiːn]	*n.* fixed and regular way of doing things 例行公事；常规
almighty [ɔːl'maiti]	*adj.* having all power; powerful beyond measure 全能的；有无限权力的
manor ['mænə]	*n.* a large country house surrounded by an estate 庄园大宅
discipline ['disiplin]	*n.* a system of rules of conduct or method of practice 训练；纪律
conviction [kən'vikʃən]	*n.* firm opinion or belief 坚定的看法或信仰
utilize [juː'tilaiz]	*v.* make use of (sth.); find a use for 利用或应用
self-fulfillment [selfful'filmənt]	*n.* the fulfillment of your capacities 自我实现

Phrases and Expressions

kick out：force to leave or move out 赶走；驱逐

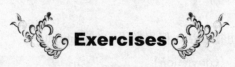

Exercises

 Comprehension of the Scene

Watch the scene carefully and answer the following questions.

1. Why does Dwayne take a vow of silence?
2. Does Frank tell the truth when asked about his arm?

3. What is grandpa complaining about?

4. How long has Dwayne been silent?

5. What does Richard think of Dwayne's vow?

6. Does Sheryl agree with Dwayne's vow?

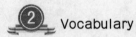 **Vocabulary**

Translate the following sentences, paying special attention to the underlined words in each pair and see the different meanings and usage of them.

1. **notice**

   A. It was Susan who brought the problem to our <u>notice</u>.

   B. Did you <u>notice</u> anything peculiar?

2. **focus**

   A. You should <u>focus</u> your attention on your work.

   B. He always wants to be the <u>focus</u> of attention.

3. **vow**

   A. Once he took the <u>vow</u>, his loyalty never wavered.

   B. He <u>vowed</u> (that) he would lose weight.

 **Translation**

Translate the following sentences into English with the help of the words in the brackets.

1. 孩子们在学校里很快活，但很散漫。（discipline）

2. 我深信我会赢。（conviction）

3. 我们必须在我们日常公务中建立一些制度。（routine）

4. 我对万能的上帝发誓我要说真话。（almighty）

5. 那项发现在科学界引起极大的震动。（tremendous）

6. 她的外表引起了我的注意。（notice）

7. 在杂志里，你可以用你产品的照片。（utilize）

8. 所有士兵都发誓效忠他们的指挥官。（vow）

Scene 2

Olive is asking Frank about his accident, which is not something good for her to know in Richard's opinion.

Olive： How did it happen?

Frank： How did what happen?

Olive： Your accident.

Sheryl： Honey, here.

Frank： Oh, no, it's okay. Unless you object.

Sheryl： No, I'm pro-honesty here. I just think, you know, it's up to you.

Frank： Be my guest.

Sheryl： Olive, um, Uncle Frank didn't really have an accident. What happened was he tried to kill himself.

Olive： You did? Why?

Richard： I'm sorry. I don't think this is an appropriate conversation. Honey, let's let Uncle Frank finish his dinner, okay? Shh.

Olive： Why did you want to kill yourself?

Richard： No, don't answer the question, Frank.

Sheryl： Richard! Richard!

Richard： He's not gonna answer the question. Frank.

Frank： I wanted to kill myself...

Richard： Don't listen to him.

Frank： I was very unhappy.

Richard： He's sick in his head.

Sheryl： Richard!

Richard： I'm sorry! I don't think it's an appropriate conversation for a seven-year-old.

Sheryl： She's gonna find out anyway.

Richard： Okay.

Sheryl： Go on, Frank.

Olive：Why were you unhappy?

Frank：Um, well, there are a lot of reasons. Mainly, though, I fell in love with someone who didn't love me back.

Olive：Who?

Frank：One of my grad students. I was very much in love with him.

Olive：Him? It was a boy? You fell in love with a boy?

Frank：Yes, I did. Very much so.

Olive：That's silly.

Frank：You're right. It was silly. It was very, very silly.

Grandpa：There's another word for it.

Richard：Dad.

Olive：So, that's when you tried to kill yourself?

Frank：Well, no. The boy that I was in love with fell in love with another man, Larry Sugarman.

Sheryl：Who's Larry Sugarman?

Frank：Larry Sugarman is, perhaps the second most highly regarded Proust scholar in the U. S.

Richard：Who's number one?

Frank：That would be me, Rich.

Richard：Really? Mm-hmm.

Olive：So that's when.

Frank：No. What happened was I was a bit upset so I said some things that I shouldn't have said and I did some things that I shouldn't have done and subsequently I was fired from my job... and forced to move out of my apartment and move into a motel.

Olive：And that's when you tried to...

Frank：Well, no. Actually, all of that was okay. What happened was two days ago the MacArthur Foundation, in its infinite wisdom awarded a genius grant to Larry Sugarman. And that's when I...

Grandpa：Decided to check out early.

Frank: Yes. Yes. And I failed at that as well.

Richard: Olive, the important thing to understand here is that Uncle Frank gave up on himself. He made a series of foolish choices. . . I'm sorry. . . and he gave up on himself which is something winners never do.

Sheryl: So that's the story, okay? Now, everyone, just let's move on and, uh. . .

Frank: Is he always like this? How can you stand it?

New Words

appropriate [ə'prəupri:ət] *adj.* suitable; right and proper 适当的；合适的；正当的

subsequently ['sʌbsikwəntli] *adv.* afterwards 后来

motel [məu'tel] *n.* a hotel for motorists, with space for parking cars near the rooms 汽车旅馆

foundation [faun'deiʃən] *n.* an organization set up to provide sums of money for research, charity, etc. 基金；基金会

infinite ['infinit] *adj.* without limits; endless 无限的；无穷的

grant [grɑ:nt] *n.* a thing given for a particular purpose, esp. money from the government 授予物；（尤指政府的）拨款

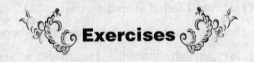

 Comprehension of the Scene

Watch the scene carefully and judge whether the following statements are TRUE or FALSE.

1. Olive was very curious about Frank's accident; however, her father didn't want her to know too much about that.

2. The fact was that Frank didn't have an accident, instead he had tried to kill himself.

3. Frank had fallen in love with someone and had been loved back.

4. Frank was actually a homosexual who had fallen in love with one of his male students.

5. Frank had been fired from his job because of his love affair with his secretary.

6. The MacArthur Foundation had awarded a genius grant to Larry Sugarman, which had been an excellent news for Frank.

7. Richard's reaction to Frank's story was well-accepted by Sheryl.

 Vocabulary

Fill in the blanks with the words given below, and change the form when necessary.

motel	upset	infinite	regard	genius
subsequently	wisdom	appropriate	silly	

1. I'm always _____ when I don't get any mail.

2. He stayed one night in a _____ and went on travelling.

3. Teaching little children takes _____ patience.

4. That _____ child never does anything; he just fools about all day long.

5. She is generally _____ as one of the best writers in the country.

6. He is not a man with worldly _____.

7. He said he was a doctor, but it _____ emerged that he was an impostor.

8. He is not so much a _____ as a hard worker.

9. Upon reaching an _____ age, children are encouraged, but not forced, to "leave the nest".

3 Oral Practice

What are true things about Frank? Tick the right answers.

A. He was actually a homosexual.

B. He had just had a car accident.

C. He was the second most highly regarded Proust scholar in the U. S.

D. He almost committed suicide.

E. He fell in love with one of his students, but this turned out to be his one-sided love.

F. He tried to kill Larry Sugarman, but failed.

G. He had been kicked out of his apartment and had to stay in a motel for a while.

H. He decided to kill himself out of jealous when the MacArthur Foundation awarded a genius grant to Larry Sugarman.

Scene 3

The family get the news that Olive is invited to the "Little Miss Sunshine" pageant and is discussing who should go with her.

Richard: You know, actually, there is a message from Cindy on the machine. Something about Little Miss Sunshine.

Olive: What? Little Miss Sunshine?

Richard: Yeah.

Olive: What?

[Woman On Machine] Sheryl, it's Cindy. Remember when Olive was here last month? She was runner-up in the regional Little Miss Sunshine? They just called right now and said that the girl who won had to forfeit her crown. I don't know why. Something about diet pills. Now she has a place in the state contest in Redondo Beach!

Olive: Oh, my gosh! I won! I won! I won! I won!

Richard: Finish your dinner!

Olive: I'm finished!

Grandpa: What happened?

Sheryl: I'm just calling to... Cindy! Yeah, we just got it. Yeah, she basically went crazy.

Olive: I won! I won! I won!

Sheryl: No, I didn't get that. The machine cut you off. Okay. Redondo Beach. This Sunday? Are you guys going?

Richard: Yes.

Sheryl: Can you put it off?

Richard: They have to. They have to.

Sheryl: Where does that leave us?

Richard: We can't do it. We can't.

Sheryl: No, no, I understand that, Cindy. Yeah.

Richard: They...

Sheryl: I just... No, I'll just figure it out. Okay, bye-bye.

Richard: It's this Sunday? Why can't Jeff and Cindy take her?

Sheryl: They have some equestrian thing in Santa Barbara.

Richard: You know, they do that horse shit every single weekend.

Sheryl: Well, it's the nationals. They're taking both horses, so apparently it's a big deal.

Richard: What about Olive?

Olive: Little Miss Sunshine! Little Miss Sunshine! I won! I won! I'm going! We're going!

Richard: You promised?

Sheryl: We'll fly out and come back on Monday.

Richard: How are you gonna get around out there?

Sheryl: We'll rent a car.

Richard: And stay at a hotel?

Sheryl: We can afford it.

Richard: This is our seed money.

Sheryl: Well, if I had a little help, bring it in.

Richard: Don't start that.

Sheryl: It all goes to your nine steps!

Richard: I told you I'm gonna talk to Stan Grossman! We're gonna get locked and loaded on this deal and start generating some income! But in the meantime we've gotta be...

Sheryl: Okay, okay! We'll drive!

Grandpa: I'm not drivin'.

Richard: How are you gonna fit Grandpa in the Miata?

Sheryl: Well, grandpa does not have to come.

Grandpa: What? I coached her! I gave her the moves. I'm gotta go.

Richard: Why don't you take the V. W. ?

Sheryl: I cannot drive a shift. I tried. We'll fly there.

Richard: We can't afford it.

Sheryl: Well, that's what we're gonna do unless you have a better idea. Here. This is dessert.

Olive: I won. I won. Little Miss Sunshine.

Richard: All right. I'll drive the bus.

Sheryl: Richard, I was told explicitly not to leave Frank by himself. No offense, Frank.

Frank:　　　None taken.

Richard:　　You got Dwayne here. They can look after each other.

Sheryl:　　 No, Richard! That's asking too much. If something happened...

Richard:　　We can't go, then, unless Dwayne and Frank go with us.

Olive:　　　Mom, where's my bathing suit?

Richard:　　Right.

Sheryl:　　 Frank?

Olive:　　　I found it!

Frank:　　　Okay.

Olive:　　　I'm going! I'm going! I'm going!

Sheryl:　　 Oh, Dwayne, come on, please. Think of your sister.

Richard:　　Come on, Dwayne. It'll be a lot of fun. You can go to the beach.

Frank:　　　This is unfair. All I ask is that you leave me alone.

Sheryl:　　 Dwayne, flight school. I will give you permission for flight school.

Olive:　　　I won! I won! I won! I won! I'm gonna win this one too!

Dwayne:　　But I'm not going to have any fun.

Frank:　　　Yeah, we're all with you on that one, Dwayne.

Olive:　　　Grandpa! Grandpa! Is Grandpa coming to California?

Sheryl:　　 We're all coming, honey.

New Words

runner-up ['rʌnə'ʌp]　　　　　*n.* the competitor who finishes second 比赛亚军

forfeit ['fɔːfit]　　　　　　　*v.* lose or give up sth. as a consequence of or punishment for having done sth. wrong 因做错事而失去或放弃

equestrian [i'kwestriən]   *adj.* of horse-riding 骑马的

generate ['dʒenəˌreit]   *v.* cause sth. to exist or occur; pro-
                                 duce 使某物存在或发生；产生

coach [kəutʃ]   *v.* teach or train sb., esp. for an
                                 examination or a sporting contest 辅
                                 导或训练某人
                                 n. bus (usu. with a single deck)
                                 for carrying passengers over long
                                 distances 长途公共汽车（通常指单
                                 层的）

shift [ʃift]   *n.* (period of time) worked by a
                                 group of workers which starts work
                                 as another group finishes 轮班职工；
                                 轮值的班

dessert [di'zə:t]   *n.* any sweet dish, (e.g. pie, tart,
                                 ice-cream) eaten at the end of a meal
                                 甜食

explicitly [ik'splisitli]   *adv.* in a precise and clear manner
                                 明白地；明确地

Phrases and Expressions

cut off：make a break in 切断

put off：postpone or cancel a meeting or an engagement with sb. 推迟或取
消会议或与某人的约会

leave sb. alone：allow one to be by oneself 不干涉某人

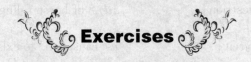

Exercises

  Comprehension of the Scene

Watch the scene carefully and answer the following questions.

1. What was Cindy's message about?

2. Would Cindy go to the Redondo Beach with Olive? Why?

3. What was Sheryl's plan at the very start? Did Richard agree with her? Why?

4. Why did grandpa say that he should go?

5. Why did Sheryl insist on Frank's going with them?

6. Why did Dwayne agree to come at last?

7. What was Sheryl's final decision?

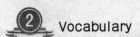 Vocabulary

Fill in the blanks with words or phrases from the scene you have just seen that match the meanings in the column on the right.

_____	the competitor who finishes second
_____	lose or give up sth. as a consequence of or punishment for having done sth. wrong
_____	of horse-riding
_____	cause (sth.) to exist or occur; produce
_____	teach or train sb., esp. for an examination or a sporting contest
_____	(period of time) worked by a group of workers which starts work as another group finishes
_____	any sweet dish
_____	in a precise and clear manner

_____ act of allowing sb. to do sth. ; consent

 Oral Practice

If you were Sheryl, would you have any other methods or plans of taking Olive to "Little Miss Sunshine?" How would you go there? Who would you take with? Why? Discuss with your partner and take notes, then make a report in the class.

Scene 4

The whole family is having breakfast in a restaurant.

Olive: Mom, how much can we spend?

Sheryl: I would say four dollars. Anything under four dollars.

Waitress: Hi. You're ready?

Richard: Yeah, I'm gonna have the, uh, number five with coffee, please.

Waitress: All right.

Sheryl: A number seven, over easy, and a grapefruit juice.

Waitress: Grapefruit. Okay.

Frank: I would like a fruit plate. And do you have chamomile?

Waitress: Yes.

Frank: With honey, please.

Grandpa: I would like the lumberjack and coffee, and extra bacon.

Richard: Extra. Now, Dad, you should probably...

Sheryl: Richard, don't start.

Richard: He's gonna kill himself.

Sheryl: Well, it's his life.

Grandpa: Thank you, Sheryl.

Waitress: Garden salad? And you?

Olive: I... I'm sorry. I, um... Sorry.

Waitress: Take your time.

Richard：	Don't apologize, Olive. It's a sign of weakness.
Olive：	Um, well, I want... Okay, okay. I know what I want. I know. Okay, can I get the waffles and, uh... I don't... What does "alamodey" mean?
Waitress：	Oh, that means it comes with ice cream.
Olive：	Okay, "alamodey" then.
Sheryl：	Olive, for breakfast?
Olive：	You said four dollars.
Sheryl：	Okay. You're right. Thank you.
Waitress：	Okay. Be right back.
Frank：	Actually, Olive, "A la mode" in French translates literally as "in the fashion". A la mode. "Mode" is derived from Latin modus, meaning "due or proper measure".
Richard：	Frank, shut up.
Sheryl：	Richard!
Richard：	Olive, can I tell you a little about ice cream?
Olive：	Yeah.
Richard：	Well, ice cream is made from cream which comes from cow's milk and cream has a lot of fat in it.
Sheryl：	Richard.
Richard：	What? She's gonna find out anyway, remember?
Olive：	What? Find out what?
Richard：	Well, when you eat ice cream, the fat in the ice cream becomes fat in your body.
Sheryl：	Richard, I swear to God!
Richard：	It's true.
Olive：	What? What's wrong?
Sheryl：	Nothing, honey. Nothing's wrong.
Richard：	So if you eat a lot of ice cream, you might become fat. And if you don't, you're gonna stay nice and skinny, sweetie.
Olive：	Mom!

Grandpa：　Olive, Richard is an idiot. I like a woman with meat on her bones.

Olive：　I don't... Why's everyone so upset?

Sheryl：　No, no one's upset, honey. I... I just want you to understand it's okay to be skinny, and it's okay to be fat, if that's what you want to be. Whatever you want, it's okay.

Richard：　Okay, but, Olive, let me ask you this. Those women in Miss America, are they skinny, or are they fat? Honey?

Olive：　Well, they're skinny, I guess.

Richard：　Yeah. I guess they don't eat a lot of ice cream.

New Words

grapefruit ['greipfruːt]	*n.* large round yellow citrus fruit with acid juicy flesh 葡萄柚
chamomile ['kæməmail]	*n.* a plant apple-scented foliage and white-rayed flowers and feathery leaves used medicinally 甘菊；黄春菊
waffle ['wɒfl]	*n.* a small crisp cake made of cooked batter with a pattern of squares on it, often eaten with syrup 华夫饼
literally ['litərəli]	*adv.* exactly 精确地
fat [fæt]	*n.* white or yellow greasy substance found in animal bodies under the skin 脂肪；肥肉
skinny ['skini]	*adj.* very thin 皮包骨的

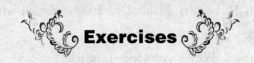

Exercises

  Comprehension of the Scene

Watch the scene carefully and answer the following questions.

1. How much can each person spend on the meal?

2. What do they order respectively?

3. What does "alamodey" mean?

4. How does Richard explain ice cream to Olive?

5. Why does grandpa call him "an idiot" when Richard doesn't allow Olive to eat ice cream?

  Vocabulary

Match the words in the left column with their corresponding meanings in the right column. Then compare with your partner.

1. bacon
A. large round yellow citrus fruit with acid juicy flesh

2. literally
B. salted or smoked meat from the back or sides of a pig

3. fat
C. say one is sorry

4. skinny
D. small crisp cake made of cooked batter with a pattern of squares on it, often eaten with syrup

5. waffle
E. exactly

6. apologize
F. white or yellow greasy substance found in animal bodies under the skin

7. grapefruit
G. very thin

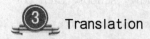 **Translation**

Translate the following sentences into Chinese.

1. I would say four dollars. Anything under four dollars.

2. Don't apologize, Olive. It's a sign of weakness.

3. Can I tell you something about ice cream?

4. Ice cream is made from cream which comes from cow's milk and cream has a lot of fat in it.

5. So if you eat a lot of ice cream, you might become fat. And if you don't, you're gonna stay nice and skinny, sweetie.

6. I don't... Why's everyone so upset?

Scene 5

Frank has his first real conversation with Dwayne.

Dwayne: Sometimes I just wish I could go to sleep till I was 18 and skip all this crap high school and everything, just skip it.

Frank: You know Marcel Proust?

Dwayne: He's the guy you teach.

Frank: Yeah. French writer. Total loser. Never had a real job. Unrequited love affairs. Gay. Spent 20 years writing a book almost no one reads. But he's also probably the greatest writer since Shakespeare. Anyway, he, he gets down to the end of his life and he looks back and decides that all those years he suffered. Those were the best years of his life, 'cause they made him who he was. All the years he was happy. You know, total waste. Didn't learn a thing. So, if you sleep until you're 18, ah, think of the suffering you're gonna miss. I mean, high school? High school, those are your prime suffering years. You don't get better suffering than that.

Dwayne: You know what? Fuck beauty contests. Life is one fucking beauty contest after another. You know, school, then college, then work? Fuck that. And fuck the Air Force Academy. If I wanna fly, I'll find a way to fly. You do what you love, and fuck the rest.

Frank: I'm glad you're talkin' again, Dwayne. You're not nearly as stupid as you look. Wanna go back?

Dwayne: Not really. Yeah, we should go back.

New Words

skip [skip]　　　　　　　　*v.* move lightly and quickly, esp. by taking two steps with each foot in turn 轻快地跳

unrequited ['ʌnri'kwaitid]　　*adj.* (esp. of love) not returned or rewarded（尤指爱情）得不到回应或报答的

prime [praim]　　　　　　　*adj.* most important; chief; fundamental 最重要的；主要的

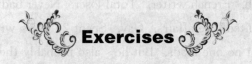 **Exercises**

 Comprehension of the Scene

Watch the scene carefully and judge whether the following statements are TRUE or FALSE.

1. Dwayne wished he could go to sleep till he was 18 because he wanted to skip many things, such as his high school.

2. Frank shared many comments with Marcel Proust, the guy he taught.

3. Proust was a French scholar, whose main research subject was

Shakespeare's works.

4. Frank totally agreed with Proust's opinion that the worst years of one's life might also be his best years of life.

5. Dwayne was actually a normal boy. He didn't speak because he had too much hatred towards life.

6. Seeing Dwayne talking again, Frank showed kind of indifference instead of happiness.

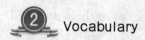 Vocabulary

Fill in the blanks with the words given below, and change the form when necessary.

| loser | prime | suffering | skip | unrequited |

1. Children are fond of _____.

2. Disappointment was written large on the face of the _____.

3. His _____ love to the girl seemed like a joke in her eyes.

4. To some life means pleasure, to others _____.

5. What was said was of _____ importance.

3 Oral Practice

What are true things about Marcel Proust? Tick the right answers.

A. He was a very famous French writer.

B. He was a gay with unrequited love affairs.

C. He had been well-accepted by readers all over the world in his time.

D. He was the greatest writer in all times.

E. He thought the worst years of his life were also the best years of his life, because they made him who he was.

F. He died in youth, leaving behind large numbers of great works.

Reading

The Script of *Little Miss Sunshine*

Michael Arndt developed the rough draft of the script in three days and later sold the completed script to producers for $150,000.

The script was written by Michael Arndt and was originally about an East Coast road trip film from Maryland to Florida, but was shifted to a journey from New Mexico to California due to budget issues. Arndt started the script on May 23, 2000 and completed the first rough draft by May 26. He had initially planned on shooting the film himself by raising several thousand dollars and using a camcorder. Instead, he gave the screenplay to producers Ron Yerxa and Albert Berger who teamed up with Deep River Productions to find a potential director.

The producers met directors Dayton and Faris while producing Election and in turn gave the script to them to read in 2001. The directors commented later on the script stating: "This film really struck a chord. We felt like it was written for us." The script was purchased from first-time screenwriter Arndt for $150,000 by Marc Turtletaub, one of the film's producers, on December 21, 2001. Yerxa and Berger remained as producers as they were responsible for finding the directors and cinematographer, assisting in the ending re-shoot, and helping bring the film to the Sundance Film Festival.

The film was pitched to several studios, and the only interested studio was Focus Features who wanted to film it in Canada. After the studio attempted to have the film be more centered on the character Richard Hoover, and Arndt disagreed, he was fired and replaced by another writer.

The new writer added several scenes, including Richard's confrontation with the character who dismisses his motivational technique business. A corporate change brought in a new studio head and Arndt was rehired when the new writer left after four weeks of rewriting the script. After two years of pre-production, Focus Features dropped the film in August 2004. Marc Turtletaub paid $400,000 to Focus Features to buy back the rights to the film and for development costs. He also paid for the 8 million budget, allowing *Little Miss Sunshine* to be filmed then.

New Words

camcorder ['kʌmkɔːdə(r)] *n.* a portable video camera with a built-in video recorder 摄像录像机

initially [i'niʃəli] *adv.* at the beginning; at first 最初；开头

comment ['kɔment] *v.* make comments; give one's opinion 评论；发表意见

chord [kɔːd] *n.* (in music) combination of notes usu. sounded together in harmony （音乐的）和弦、和音

confrontation [ˌkɔnfrʌn'teiʃən] *n.* (instance of) angry opposition 对抗；对抗的事物

dismiss [dis'mis] *v.* remove sb. (esp. an employee) from a position 免除某人（尤指雇员）的职务；开除

cinematographer [ˌsinimə'tɔgrəfə] *n.* a photographer who operates a movie camera 电影摄影师

Reading Comprehension

Read this article carefully and answer the following questions.

1. Who developed the rough draft of the script and how long did it take him?

2. What did Arndt plan to do with the script at the very start?

3. How did the directors like the script when they read it for the first time?

4. Was the script popular among studios?

5. Why was Arndt fired by the Focus Features?

Chapter Four

The Chronicles of Narnia:Prince Caspian

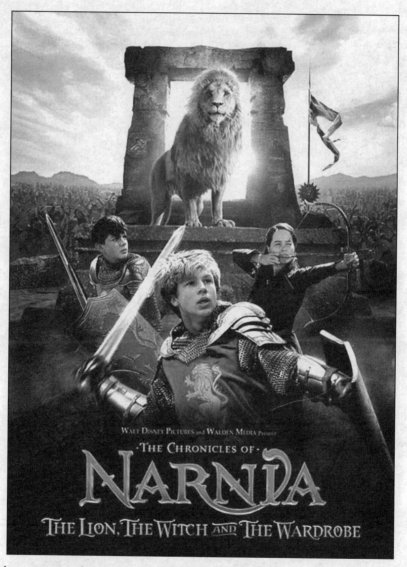

Things never happen the same way twice.

Main Characters

Prince Caspian.............................Ben Barnes
Lucy Pevensie............................Georgie Henley
Peter Pevensie...........................William Mosely
Edmund Pevensie.........................Skandar Keynes
Susan Pevensie..........................Anna Popplewell

Warming-up

Synopsis

Peter, Susan, Edmund and Lucy are transposed from a country railway station to an island in Narnia when young Prince Caspian X — who is heir to the throne at Cair Paravel, and is in danger in a battle against the Telmarine siege  of Narnia — has blown Queen Susan's magic horn. King Miraz (Caspian's Uncle), a tyrant who murdered Caspian's father (Caspian IX), has claimed the throne. After Miraz's wife Queen Prunaprismia gave birth to a son, Miraz planned to kill off Caspian X. However, young Prince Caspian managed to escape into Old Narnia and unite with "the creatures that lived in

hiding". With the help of the centaur Glenstorm, Trufflehunter (a loyal badger), Trumpkin (a skeptical but dedicated dwarf), Reepicheep (a valiant mouse) and scores of other species of friendly Narnian animals, Caspian forms an army to meet Miraz's countless, mighty human warriors.

In an early battle, the Narnians make strategic mistakes, many animals die, and they are forced to retreat. Trumpkin intercepts the Pevensies shortly after their arrival at the ruins of Cair Paravel（once a peninsula — now the island they were summoned to when Caspian sounded Queen Susan's horn）. As they travel toward Aslan's How （the location of the destroyed Stone Table — now an under-

ground fortress, and the loyal Narnians' defense）, the war between good and evil escalates. A rebel Narnian dwarf harbors enemies, Aslan appears to Lucy, and the Pevensies finally unite with Caspian.

High King Peter drafts a challenge, which King Edmund presents to the Lords Glozelle and Sopespian. Angered by his counsel's subtle（but intentional）doubt of his bravery, King Miraz insists on accepting the challenge. With both armies surrounding them on the Beruna landscape, Miraz and Peter draw swords and duel fiercely.

In a moment of the fight, Miraz is knocked to the ground. Astoundingly, his own lords stab him in the back and then shout out that Peter has killed him egregiously. All at once an immense battle amasses — the Second Battle of Beruna — as the Telmarines and the Narnians fight for autonomy of the land.

In the culmination of the battle, Aslan renews the land. He calls forth the dryads（tree spirits）to dance again; he awakens the river god, who then destroys a massive man-made wooden bridge over the Fjords of Beruna; and he beckons Bacchus and Silenus, and their merry maidens, who run throughout the landscape as far as the town of Beaversdam celebrating.

In Prince Caspian, humans had come to constitute a large portion of the population in Narnia. But in the Golden Age of Narnia, when the Pevensies fulfilled a prophecy by taking throne, they were the only humans in Narnia. Aslan tells Caspian how his ancestors came into Narnia. He reveals that they actually originated from the same Earth as the Pevensies. Years ago, pirates in the "South Sea" (of our world) came upon an island, and, after entering a cave, fell (through a chasm) into Telmar. Telmar is the country to the West of Narnia. After many years in Narnian time, the Telmarines, who suffered famine and internal conflict, invaded and sieged Narnia. During this time, the animals of Narnia fled into hiding, as the human Telmarines came to dominate the land. Prince Caspian was the tenth in a line of kings by that name.

New Words

transpose [træns'pəuz]　　　　*v.* cause two or more things to change places 使物体互换位置

tyrant ['taiərənt]　　　　　　*n.* a cruel, unjust or oppressive ruler, esp. one who has obtained complete power by force 暴虐的统治者，尤指武力夺权者

skeptical ['skeptikəl]　　　　*adj.* denying or questioning the tenets of especially a religion 怀疑的

dedicated ['dedikeitid]　　　　*adj.* devoted to sth.; committed 献身于某事物的；专心致志的

valiant ['væljənt]　　　　　　*adj.* brave or determined 勇敢的

intercept [ˌintə'sept]　　　　*v.* stop or catch sb. travelling or sth. in motion before he or it can reach a destination 中途阻止或拦截

peninsula [piˈninsjulə]	*n.* area of land almost surrounded by water or projecting far into the sea 半岛
fortress [ˈfɔːtris]	*n.* castle or large fort; town strengthened against attack 城堡或大的碉堡
escalate [ˈeskəleit]	*v.* (cause sth. to) increase or develop by successive stages 逐步增长或发展
sword [sɔːd]	*n.* weapon with a long thin metal blade and a protected handle（用作武器，有防护手柄的）剑
duel [ˈdjuːəl]	*n.* (formerly) formal fight between two men, using swords or pistols, esp. to settle a point of honour（旧时）两男子的决斗，用剑或手枪，尤指关系到名誉问题
stab [stæb]	*v.* pierce (sth.) or wound (sb.) with a pointed tool or weapon 戳（某物）；刺伤（某人）
egregiously [iˈɡriːdʒəsli]	*adv.* exceptionally; outstandingly 异乎寻常地；突出地
amass [əˈmæs]	*v.* gather together or collect sth. (esp. in large quantities)（尤指大量地）积累；积聚
culmination [kʌlmiˈneiʃən]	*n.* eventual conclusion or result 结局；结果

beckon ['bekən]

v. make a gesture to sb. with the hand, arm or head, usu. to make him come nearer or to follow（以手、臂或头部的动作）召唤某人（通常为使之走近或跟随自己）

prophecy ['prɔfisi]

n. (power of) saying what will happen in the future 预言

chasm ['kæzəm]

n. deep opening in the ground; abyss; gorge 深坑；深渊

famine ['fæmin]

n. extreme scarcity of food in a region 饥荒

Read the synopsis carefully and answer the following questions.

1. Who is Prince Caspian X?
2. Who did Prince Caspian's army include?
3. What is Aslan's How?
4. Who killed King Miraz?
5. According to Aslan, how did people's ancestors come into Narnia?

Scene Study

Scene 1

The Pevensie brothers found Cair Paravel and tried to get into it.

Edmund: Catapults.

Peter: What?

Edmund: This didn't just happen. Cair Paravel was attacked.

Peter: Don't suppose you have any matches, here.

Edmund: No, but would this help?

Peter: You might have mentioned that a bit sooner. I can't believe it. It's all still here.

Lucy: I was so tall.

Susan: Well, you were older then.

Edmund: As opposed to hundreds of years later when you're younger.

Lucy: What is it?

Susan: My horn. I must've left it on my saddle the day we went back.

Peter: When Aslan bares his teeth, winter meets its death.

Lucy: When he shakes his mane, we shall have spring again. Eve-ryone we knew... Mr. Tumnus and the Beavers... they're all gone.

Peter: I think it's time we found out what's going on.

Soldier 1: He won't stop staring.

Soldier 2: So don't look.

Soldier 1: Here's far enough.

Susan: Drop him!

Trumpkin: Crows and crockery! "Drop him"! That's the best you can come up with?

Susan:	A simple "thank you" would suffice.
Trumpkin:	They were doing fine drowning me without your help.
Peter:	Maybe we should have let them.
Lucy:	Why were they trying to kill you, anyway?
Trumpkin:	They're Telmarines. That's what they do.
Edmund:	Telmarines? In Narnia?
Trumpkin:	Where have you been for the last few hundred years?
Lucy:	It's a bit of a long story.
Trumpkin:	Oh, you've got to be kidding me. You're it? You're the kings and queens of old?
Peter:	High King Peter, the Magnificent.
Susan:	You probably could've left off the last bit.
Trumpkin:	Probably.
Peter:	You might be surprised.
Trumpkin:	You don't want to do that, boy.
Peter:	Not me. Him.
Susan:	Edmund!
Trumpkin:	You all right? Oh! Beards and bedsteads! Maybe that horn worked after all.
Susan:	What horn?

New Words

catapult ['kætəpʌlt]   *n.* (in ancient times) machine for throwing heavy stones in war （古时）投石器

saddle ['sædl]   *n.* (a) seat, often of leather, for a rider on a horse, donkey, etc. or on a bicycle or motor cycle 鞍；（自行车

或摩托车的）车座

bare [bɛə]　　　　　　　　*v.* uncover (sth.); reveal 使裸露出来；揭开

mane [mein]　　　　　　　*n.* long hair on the neck of a horse, lion, etc. （马等的）鬃；（狮等的）鬣

crow [krəu]　　　　　　　*n.* any of various types of large black bird with a harsh cry 乌鸦

crockery ['krɔkəri]　　　*n.* cups, plates, dishes, etc. made of baked clay 陶器；瓦器

suffice [sə'fais]　　　　　*v.* be enough for sb. /sth. ; be adequate 能满足某人/某物需要的；足够的

bedstead ['bedsted]　　　*n.* framework of wood or metal supporting the springs and mattress of a bed 床架

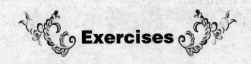 **Exercises**

 Comprehension of the Scene

Watch the scene carefully and answer the following questions.

1. What do the catapults mean in this scene?
2. Why was Susan's horn in the case?
3. Who saved the dwarf?
4. Who tried to kill the dwarf?
5. Who are the Pevensie brothers?

Vocabulary and Structure

Fill in the blanks with the words given below, and change the form when necessary.

saddle	stare	bare	suffice
magnificent	catapult	mane	crow

1. The _____ croaked disaster.
2. What a _____ sight!
3. They all _____ at him with astonishment.
4. Better lose the _____ than the horse.
5. The car stopped suddenly and I was _____ through the windshield.
6. The strongest man that you can think of cannot tear the log apart with _____ hands.
7. The food will _____ until next week.
8. Angry animals erect the _____ .

Translation

Translate the following sentences into English and use the words or expressions given in the brackets.

1. 这个小房间几乎没有什么家具。(be bare of)
2. 老人把不速之客上下打量了一番。(stare)
3. 乌鸦是不祥的预兆。(crow)
4. 她的收入足够她用。(suffice for)
5. 我们参观了一座城里的宏伟宫殿。(magnificent)

Scene 2

The Prince Caspian was walking in the forest.

Caspian: I can hear you.

Trufflehunter: I just think we should wait for the kings and queens.

Nikabrik: Fine! Go then! See if the others will be as understanding! Or maybe I'll come with you. I want to see you explain things to the minotaurs.

Caspian: Minotaurs? They're real?

Trufflehunter: And very bad-tempered.

Nikabrik: Yeah, not to mention big.

Trufflehunter: Huge.

Caspian: What about centaurs? Do they still exist?

Trufflehunter: Well, the centaurs will probably fight on your side. But there's no telling what the others will do.

Caspian: What about Aslan?

Nikabrik: How do you know so much about us?

Caspian: Stories.

Trufflehunter: Wait a minute. Your father told you stories about Narnia?

Caspian: No, my professor. Listen, I'm sorry. These are not the kind of questions you should be asking.

Nikabrik: What is it?

Trufflehunter: Human.

Nikabrik: Him?

Trufflehunter: No. Them.

Soldiers: There they are!

Caspian: Run!

Soldiers: Now!

Nikabrik: Oh, no.

Caspian: Wait. I'll go.

Trufflehunter：Take it. Go! It's more important than I am.

Caspian：Get him out of here.

Soldier：Where are you?

Reepicheep：Choose your last words carefully, Telmarine.

Caspian：You are a mouse.

Reepicheep：I was hoping for something a little more original. Pick up your sword.

Caspian：No, thanks.

Reepicheep：Pick it up! I will not fight an unarmed man.

Caspian：Which is why I might live longer if I choose not to cross blades with you, noble mouse.

Reepicheep：I said I would not fight you. I didn't say I'd let you live!

Trufflehunter：Reepicheep! Stay your blade!

Reepicheep：Trufflehunter? I trust you have a very good reason for this untimely interruption.

Nikabrik：He doesn't. Go ahead.

Trufflehunter：He's the one who blew the horn.

Reepicheep：What?

Centaur：Then let him bring it forward. This is the reason we have gathered.

Narnians：Kill him! Telmarine! Liar! Murderer!

Dwarf：All this horn proves is they've stolen yet another thing from us!

Caspian：I didn't steal anything.

Minotaur：Didn't steal anything? Shall we list the things the Telmarines have taken?

Narnians：Our homes! Our land! Our freedom! Our lives! You stole Narnia!

Caspian：You would hold me accountable for all the crimes of my people?

Dwarf:	Accountable... and punishable.
Reepicheep:	That is rich coming from you, dwarf. Have you forgotten it was your people who fought alongside the White Witch?
Dwarf:	And I'd gladly do it again, if it would rid us of these barbarians.
Trufflehunter:	Then it's lucky that it is not in your power to bring her back. Or are you suggesting that we ask this boy to go against Aslan now? Some of you may have forgotten, but we badgers remember well, that Narnia was never right except when a Son of Adam was king.
Dwarf:	He's a Telmarine! Why would we want him as our king?
Caspian:	Because I can help you.
Narnians:	It's a trick! At least hear him out!
Caspian:	Beyond these woods, I'm a prince. The Telmarine throne is rightfully mine! Help me claim it, and I can bring peace between us.
Centaur:	It is true. The time is ripe. I watch the skies, for it is mine to watch as it is yours to remember, badger. Tarva, the lord of victory, and Alambil, the lady of peace, have come together in the high heavens. And now here, a Son of Adam has come forth to offer us back our freedom.
Squirrel:	Is this possible? Do you really think there could be peace? Do you? I mean, really?
Caspian:	Two days ago, I didn't believe in the existence of talking animals or dwarves or centaurs. Yet here you are in strength and numbers that we Telmarines could never have imagined. Whether this horn is magic or not, it brought us together. And together, we have a chance to take back what is ours.
Centaur:	If you will lead us, then my sons and I offer you our swords.

Reepicheep: And we offer you our lives, unreservedly.

Trufflehunter: Miraz's army will not be far behind us, Sire.

Caspian: If we are to be ready for them, we need to hurry to find soldiers and weapons. I'm sure they will be here soon.

New Words

unarmed [ˈʌnˈɑːmd]   *adj.* without weapons 无武器的；未武装的

blade [bleid]   *n.* flat cutting part of a knife, sword, chisel, etc. （刀、剑、凿等的）刃

untimely [ʌnˈtaimli]   *adj.* happening at an unsuitable time 不适时的；不合时宜的

crime [kraim]   *n.* offence for which one may be punished by law 罪；罪行

barbarian [bɑːˈbɛəriən]   *adj.* a person who is primitive, coarse or cruel 野蛮的、粗鲁的或残忍的人

trick [trik]   *n.* things done in order to deceive or outwit sb. 诡计；花招

unreservedly [ˈʌnriˈzɜːvidli]   *adv.* without being saved for future use or restriction 无保留地；无限制地

Phrases and Expressions

not to mention: much less, let along 更不用说

be accountable for：be responsible for 对······应负责任

Exercises

 Comprehension of the Scene

Watch the scene carefully and answer the following questions.

1. Who told Prince Caspian the stories of Narnia?

2. Who saved them in the forest?

3. Why did Narnians want to kill Prince Caspian?

4. Why did Centaur agree to help Caspian?

5. What brought them together?

 Vocabulary and Structure

Fill in the blanks with the words given below，and change the form when necessary.

trick	ripe	weapon	throne
original	blade	crime	barbarian

1. He is an _____ dramatist.

2. Daily practice is the _____ in learning a foreign language.

3. He committed a high _____ .

4. The time is _____ for a new foreign policy.

5. Who is first in succession to the _____ ?

6. They were testing a new _____ then.

7. There is a _____ tribe living in this forest.

8. The _____ needs sharpening.

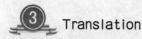 **3** Translation

Translate the following sentences into English and use the words or expressions given in the brackets.

1. 你现在出去踢足球太晚了，何况又正在下雨。（not to mention）

2. 每个人都要对自己的工作负责。（be accountable for）

3. 我们不相信真有鬼。（existence）

4. 那条船在码头旁停靠。（alongside）

5. 他那不合时宜的干涉让我生气。（untimely）

Scene 3

The Pevensie brothers tried to find the way to Narnia, but they found they encountered the army of their enemy, the Telmarine, so they chose another way. At night, they rested in the forest.

Susan: Lucy, are you awake? Why do you think I didn't see Aslan?

Lucy: You believe me?

Susan: Well, we got across the gorge.

Lucy: I don't know. Maybe you didn't really want to.

Susan: You always knew we'd be coming back here, didn't you?

Lucy: I hoped so.

Susan: I finally just got used to the idea of being in England.

Lucy: But you're happy to be here, aren't you?

Susan: While it lasts.

Aslan: Lucy. Lucy.

Lucy: Aslan! I've missed you so much! You've grown.

Aslan: Every year you grow, so shall I.

Lucy: Where have you been? Why haven't you come to help us?

Aslan: Things never happen the same way twice, dear one.

Lucy: Susan! Wake up!

Susan:	Certainly, Lu. Whatever you like.
Lucy:	Wake up. Aslan? No, stop!
Peter:	Prince Caspian?
Caspian:	Yes? And who are you?
Susan:	Peter!
Caspian:	High King Peter.
Peter:	I believe you called.
Caspian:	Well, yes, but I thought you'd be older.
Peter:	If you like, we could come back in a few years.
Caspian:	No. No, that's all right. You're just... you're not exactly what I expected.
Edmund:	Neither are you.
Trufflehunter:	A common enemy unites even the oldest of foes.
Reepicheep:	We have anxiously awaited your return, my liege. Our hearts and swords are at your service.
Lucy:	Oh, my gosh, he is so cute.
Reepicheep:	Who said that?
Lucy:	Sorry.
Reepicheep:	Your Majesty, with the greatest respect, I do believe "courageous", "courteous", or "chivalrous" might more befit a knight of Narnia.
Peter:	Well, at least we know some of you can handle a blade.
Reepicheep:	Yes, indeed. And I have recently put it to good use, securing weapons for your army, sire.
Peter:	Good. Because we're going to need every sword we can get.
Caspian:	Well, then, you will probably be wanting yours back.
Miraz:	How much did they take?
Glozelle:	Enough weapons and armor for two regiments. But there's more.
Miraz:	You were right to fear the woods.

Sopespian:	X?
Miraz:	Caspian. The tenth.
Glozelle:	I apologize, my lord. The blame is mine.
Miraz:	I know. Tell me, general, how many men did you lose?
Glozelle:	None, my lord.
Miraz:	None?
Glozelle:	They came like ghosts, in the dead of night. We never saw them.
Miraz:	Then how do you explain your injuries? I asked how many men were killed during this bloody Narnian attack? Of which you were a fortunate survivor. General, how many?
Glozelle:	Three.
Miraz:	I apologize, Lord Sopespian. Caspian is not a victim of this savage uprising. He is the instigator. It seems Narnia is in need of a new king.
Peter:	Well, it's good you have troops, but we need some fortifications. Somewhere to train.
Trufflehunter:	So? What are they like?
Trumpkin:	Malcontent, complainers... Stubborn as mules in the morning...
Trufflehunter:	So you like them, then.
Trumpkin:	Well enough.
Caspian:	It may not be what you are used to, but it is defensible.
Susan:	Peter. You may want to see this. It's us.
Lucy:	What is this place?
Caspian:	You don't know?
Lucy:	He must know what he's doing.
Peter:	I think it's up to us now. It's only a matter of time. Miraz's men and war machines are on their way. That means those same men aren't protecting his castle.
Reepicheep:	What do you propose we do, Your Majesty?

Peter:	We need to get ready for it.
Caspian:	To start planning for...
Peter:	Our only hope is to strike them before they strike us.
Caspian:	But, that's crazy. No one has taken that castle.
Peter:	There's always a first time.
Trumpkin:	We'll have the element of surprise.
Caspian:	But we have the advantage here!
Susan:	If we dig in, we could probably hold them off indefinitely.
Trufflehunter:	I, for one, feel safer underground.
Peter:	Look. I appreciate what you've done here, but this isn't a fortress. It's a tomb.
Edmund:	Yes. And if they're smart, the Telmarines will just wait and starve us out.
Squirrel:	We could collect nuts!
Reepicheep:	Yes! And throw them at the Telmarines. Shut up! I think you know where I stand, sire.
Peter:	If I get your troops in, can you handle the guards?
Centaur:	Or die trying, my liege.
Lucy:	That's what I'm worried about.
Peter:	Sorry?
Lucy:	You're all acting like there's only two options. Dying here, or dying there.
Peter:	I'm not sure you've been listening.
Lucy:	No, you're not listening. Or have you forgotten who really defeated the White Witch, Peter?
Peter:	I think we've waited for Aslan long enough.

New Words

gorge ['gɔːdʒ]   *n.* narrow steep-sided valley, usu. with a stream or river 峡谷

foe [fəu]

n. enemy 敌人

courteous ['kɔːtjəs]

adj. having or showing good manners; polite 彬彬有礼的；客气的

chivalrous ['ʃivəlrəs]

adj. (in the Middle Ages) showing the qualities of a perfect knight（中世纪的）表现出完美的骑士精神的

befit [bi'fit]

v. be right and suitable for (sb.); be appropriate for 适合于（某人）；合适

secure [si'kjuə]

v. make (sth.) safe; protect 使（某事物）安全；保护

regiment ['redʒimənt]

n. (artillery and armour) unit divided into batteries or squadrons（炮兵的和装甲兵的）团

victim ['viktim]

n. a person, an animal or a thing that is injured, killed or destroyed as the result of carelessness, crime or misfortune 由于粗心、犯罪或不幸，被伤害或毁灭的人、动物或事物

savage ['sævidʒ]

adj. wild, fierce 野性的；凶猛的

instigator ['instigeitə]

n. a person who provokes or stirs up (esp. sth. bad)（尤指不好的事）教唆者、煽动者

fortification [fɔːtifi'keiʃən]

n. tower, wall, ditch, etc. built to defend a place against attack 碉堡、围墙、战壕等

malcontent ['mælkən,tent]   *adj.* discontented and rebellious 不满的；反叛的

stubborn ['stʌbən]   *adj.* determined; not to give way; strong-willed; obstinate 不退让的；倔犟的；固执的

mule [mjuːl]   *n.* animal that is the offspring of a donkey and a horse, used for carrying loads and noted for its stubbornness 骡子

defensible [di'fensəbl]   *adj.* that protect against a challenge or attack; that fight against or resist strongly 可保卫的；可防御的

indefinitely [in'definitli]   *adv.* to an unlimited extent 无限地

starve [stɑːv]   *v.* (cause a person or an animal to) suffer severely or die from hunger 挨饿；饿死

Phrases and Expressions

at one's service：serve for sb. 由……安排；随……安排

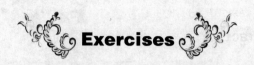

Exercises

  ## Comprehension of the Scene

Watch the scene carefully and answer the following questions.

1. Did Susan believe that Lucy saw Aslan?

2. How did Reepicheep, the mouse, describe himself?

3. How many soldiers did Miraz's army lose?

4. What's Peter's plan?

5. What's Caspian's idea?

  ## Vocabulary and Structure

Fill in the blanks with the words given below, and change the form when necessary.

knight	savage	option	starve
befit	victim	stubborn	tomb

1. He likes _____ mountain scenery.

2. He wore a sober suit that _____ the occasion.

3. The _____ of the explosion were buried last week.

4. We visited the _____ of Shakespeare.

5. The explorers _____ to death in the desert.

6. That _____ ran his sword through his foe.

7. She had no _____ but to quit her job in order to take care of her child.

8. He is as _____ as a mule.

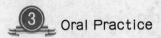 Oral Practice

What are true things according to the scene? Tick the right answers.

1. Susan is happy to be here.

2. Aslan comes to help them.

3. Peter is younger than Caspian thought.

4. No soldier died during the Narnia attack.

5. The dwarf, Trumpkin, doesn't like Narnians.

6. Edmund wants to wait in the castle.

7. Lucy agrees with Prince Caspian.

8. No one expects that Aslan will help them.

Scene 4

Miraz's army is approaching Narnia.

Peter: You're lucky, you know.

Lucy: What do you mean?

Peter: To have seen him. I wish he'd just given me some sort of proof.

Lucy: Maybe we're the ones who need to prove ourselves to him.

Edmund: Peter. You'd better come quickly.

Trumpkin: Cakes and kettledrums. That's your next big plan? Sending a little girl into the darkest parts of the forest? Alone!

Peter: It's our only chance.

Susan: And she won't be alone.

Trumpkin: Haven't enough of us died already?

Trufflehunter: Nikabrik was my friend too. But he lost hope. Queen Lucy hasn't. And neither have I.

Reepicheep: For Aslan.

Bear: For Aslan.

Trumpkin: Then I'm going with you.

Lucy:	No. We need you here.
Peter:	We have to hold them off until Lucy and Susan get back.
Caspian:	If I may... Miraz may be a tyrant and a murderer, but as a king, he is subject to the traditions and expectations of his people. There is one in particular that may buy us some time.
Glozelle:	Perhaps they intend to surrender.
Miraz:	No. They are much too noble for that.
Edmund:	I, Peter, by the gift of Aslan, by election and by conquest, High King of Narnia, Lord of Cair Paravel and emperor of the Lone Islands, in order to prevent the abominable effusion of blood, do hereby challenge the usurper Miraz to single combat upon the field of battle. The fight shall be to the death. The reward shall be total surrender.
Miraz:	Tell me, Prince Edmund...
Edmund:	King.
Miraz:	Pardon me?
Edmund:	It's King Edmund, actually. Just "King", though. Peter's the High King. I know, it's confusing.
Miraz:	Why would we risk such a proposal when our armies could wipe you out by nightfall?
Edmund:	Haven't you already underestimated our numbers? I mean, only a week ago, Narnians were extinct.
Miraz:	And so you will be again.
Edmund:	Well, then you should have little to fear.
Miraz:	This is not a question of bravery.
Edmund:	So you're bravely refusing to fight a swordsman half your age?
Miraz:	I didn't say I refused.
Lord:	You shall have our support, Your Majesty. Whatever

your decision.

Sopespian: Sire, our military advantage alone provides the perfect excuse to avoid what might otherwise be...

Miraz: I'm not avoiding anything!

Sopespian: I was merely pointing out that my lord is well within his rights to refuse.

Glozelle: His Majesty would never refuse. He relishes the chance to show the people the courage of their new king.

Miraz: You! You should hope your brother's sword is sharper than his pen.

Caspian: Destrier has always served me well. You are in good hands.

Susan: Or hooves.

Caspian: Good luck.

Susan: Thanks.

Caspian: Look. Maybe it is time you had this back.

Susan: Why don't you hold on to it? You might need to call me again.

Lucy: You might need to call me again?

Susan: Oh, shut up.

New Words

proof [pruːf]   *n.* (a piece of) evidence that shows, or helps to show, that sth. is true or is a fact 证据；证物

kettledrum ['ketldrʌm]   *n.* large brass or copper bowl-shaped drum with skin stretched over the top, that can be tuned to an exact pitch 定音鼓

surrender [sə'rendə]

v. stop resisting an enemy, etc.; yield; give up 停止抵抗；投降；屈服

conquest ['kɔŋkwest]

n. conquering; defeat 征服；击败

abominable [ə'bɔminəbl]

adj. very unpleasant 令人很不愉快的

effusion [i'fju:ʃən]

n. pouring out, esp. of liquid 倾出；流出

hereby [hiə'bai]

adv. by this means; as a result of this 以此方式；由此

usurper [ju:'zə:pə]

n. one who wrongfully or illegally seizes and holds the place of another 篡夺者

combat ['kɔmbət]

n. fight or fighting between two people, armies, etc. 格斗；搏斗

underestimate ['ʌndə'estimeit]

v. make too low an evaluate of sb. / sth. 过分低估某人/某事物

extinct [iks'tiŋkt]

adj. （esp. of a type of animal, etc.）no longer in existence（尤指动物种类等）不再存在的；绝种的

military ['militəri]

adj. of or for soldiers or an army 军人的；军队的

merely ['miəli]

adv. only; simply 只；不过

relish ['reliʃ]

n. enjoy or get pleasure out of (sth.) 享受；从（某事物）中获得乐趣

Phrases and Expressions

sort of：to some（great or small）extent 有几分地；在某种程度上

in particular：specifically or especially distinguished from others 特别；尤其

wipe out：an event（or the result of an event）that completely destroys sth. 消灭；彻底摧毁

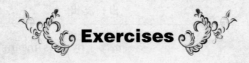

Exercises

 Comprehension of the Scene

Watch the scene carefully and answer the following questions.

1. Why does Peter think Lucy is lucky?

2. Who will go to the darkest parts of the forest?

3. Which characteristic of Miraz can buy Narnians some time?

4. Why doesn't Miraz think Narnians will surrender?

5. Does Miraz want to combat with Peter? Does he agree finally?

 Vocabulary and Structure

Fill in the blanks with the words given below，and change the form when necessary.

proof	surrender	noble	emperor
combat	military	extinct	merely

1. That was _____ a guess of mine.

2. The _____ between good and evil will continue forever.

3. I can give you more than one _____ that it is true.

4. The passenger pigeon is _____ .

5. The criminal _____ himself to the police.

6. His friend is a man of _____ mind.

7. He did a year's _____ service.

8. The _____ was actually a political eunuch.

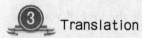 Translation

Translate the following sentences into English and use the words or expressions given in the brackets.

1. 我多少料到你也许会那么说。（sort of）

2. 她特别强调了那一点。（in particular）

3. 他们已彻底摧毁了敌人的主要军事目标。（wipe out）

4. 盒子上的使用说明含混不清。（confusing）

5. 不要低估了这项工作的艰巨性。（underestimate）

Scene 5

With the help of Aslan，the Narnians defeated King Miraz's army.

Narnians： Assemble on that bank! You will not be harmed! Surrender your weapons! Take off the armor!

Aslan： Rise，kings and queens of Narnia. All of you.

Caspian： I do not think I am ready.

Aslan： It's for that very reason I know you are.

Reepicheep： Thank you，Your Majesty. Thank you. Hail，Aslan! It is a great honor to be in... I'm completely out of countenance. I must crave your indulgence for appearing in this unseemly fashion. Perhaps a drop more?

Lucy： I don't think it does that.

Reepicheep： You could have a go.

Aslan： It becomes you well，small one.

Reepicheep: All the same, great king, I regret that I must withdraw, for a tail is the honor and glory of a mouse.

Aslan: Perhaps you think too much of your honor, friend.

Reepicheep: Well, it's not just the honor. It's also great for balance, and climbing, and grabbing things.

Mouse: May it please Your High Majesty, we will not bear the shame of wearing an honor denied to our chief.

Aslan: Not for the sake of your dignity, but for the love of your people.

Reepicheep: Look! Thank you, my liege. I will treasure it always. From this day forward it will serve as a great reminder of my huge humility.

Aslan: Now, where is this dear little friend you've told me so much about?

Lucy: Do you see him now?

Aslan: Because you have snuck in... I'm sorry, but their future in that world shall be good. Your Majesty?

Caspian: We are ready. Everyone has assembled. Narnia belongs to the Narnians, just as it does to man. Any Telmarines who want to stay and live in peace are welcome to. But for any of you who wish, Aslan will return you to the home of our forefathers.

Telmarines: It's been generations since we left Telmar.

Aslan: We're not referring to Telmar. Your ancestors were seafaring brigands. Pirates run aground on an island. There they found a cave, a rare chasm that brought them here from their world. The same world as our kings and queens. It is to that island I can return you. It is a good place for any who wish to make a new start.

Glozelle: I will go. I will accept the offer.

Queen: So will we.

Aslan: Because you have spoken first, your future in that world shall be good.

Telmarines: Where did they go? They killed them. How do we know he is not leading us to our death?

Reepicheep: Sire. If my example can be of any service, I will take 11 mice through with no delay.

Peter: We'll go.

Edmund: We will?

Peter: Come on. Our time's up. After all, we're not really needed here anymore.

Caspian: I will look after it until you return.

Susan: I'm afraid that's just it. We're not coming back.

Lucy: We're not?

Peter: You two are. At least, I think he means you two.

Lucy: But why? Did they do something wrong?

Aslan: Quite the opposite, dear one. But all things have their time. Your brother and sister have learned what they can from this world. Now it's time for them to live in their own.

Peter: It's all right, Lu. It's not how I thought it would be, but it's all right. One day you'll see, too. Come on.

Susan: I'm glad I came back.

Caspian: I wish we had more time together.

Susan: It would never have worked, anyway.

Caspian: Why not?

Susan: I am 1,300 years older than you.

Lucy: I'm sure when I'm older I'll understand.

Edmund: I'm older and don't think I want to understand.

Boy: Aren't you coming, Phyllis?

Edmund: You don't think there's any way we can get back? I've left my new torch in Narnia.

New Words

assemble [ə'sembl]　　　　　　　*v.* (cause people or things to) come together; collect 集合；聚集；收集

armor ['ɑːmə]　　　　　　　　*n.* protective covering made of metal and used in combat 盔甲；装甲

hail [heil]　　　　　　　　　　*interj.* (arch. 古) welcome! 欢迎！

countenance ['kauntinəns]　　　*n.* expression on sb.'s face 面孔；面容

crave [kreiv]　　　　　　　　　*v.* ask for sth. earnestly; beg for 恳求某事物；祈求

indulgence [in'dʌldʒəns]　　　*n.* (in the Roman Catholic Church) granting of freedom from punishment for sin (天主教会的) 特赦；赦免

unseemly [ʌn'siːmli]　　　　　*adj.* (of behaviour, etc.) not proper or seemly (指行为等) 不适当的；不适宜的

withdraw [wið'drɔː]　　　　　*v.* pull or take sb./sth. back or away 收回；撤回

glory ['glɔːri]　　　　　　　　*n.* high fame and honour won by great achievements 光荣；荣誉

dignity ['digniti]　　　　　　　*n.* quality that earns or deserves respect; true worth 高尚的品质；尊贵

humility [hjuː'militi]　　　　　*n.* humble attitude of mind; modesty 谦虚的态度；谦逊

ancestor ['ænsestə]   *n.* any of the people from whom sb. is descended，esp. those more remote than his grandparents；forefather 祖先；祖宗

seafaring ['si:. feəriŋ]   *n.* (of) work or travel on the sea 海上工作或航海的

brigand ['brigənd]   *n.* member of a band of robbers, esp. one attacking travellers in forests and mountains 强盗；土匪

pirate ['paiərit]   *n.* a person on a ship who attacks and robs other ships at sea 海盗

torch [tɔ:tʃ]   *n.* a small hand-held electric lamp powered by a battery 手电筒；电棒

Phrases and Expressions

for the sake of：for the interests of 为了……的原因
sneak in：enter surreptitiously 偷偷溜进
refer to：mean 涉及；指的是

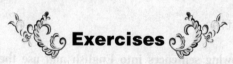 Exercises

 Comprehension of the Scene

Watch the scene carefully and answer the following questions.

1. What does Reepicheep lose during the war?
2. Who are Telmarines' forefathers?
3. Do Tel marines believe in Aslan's words?
4. Will Pevensie brothers stay in Narnia forever?

5. What does Edmund leave in Narnia?

 Vocabulary and Structure

Fill in the blanks with the words given below, and change the form when necessary.

assemble	opposite	glory	pirate
crave	dignity	humility	ancestor

1. _____ boarded the vessel and robbed the passengers.

2. The artist _____ recognition of his talents.

3. He took part in the competition for the _____ of the school.

4. Over 10,000 people were _____ at the airport to honor the President's visit.

5. He is sprung from noble _____ .

6. The girl has the great virtues of _____ and kindness.

7. They have _____ views on the question.

8. A man's _____ depends not upon his wealth but upon his character.

3 Translation

Translate the following sentences into English and use the words or expressions given in the brackets.

1. 绝不要为金钱而做坏事。(for the sake of)

2. 我看天黑后能否让他偷偷地溜进去。(sneak in)

3. 请别再提这件事。(refer to)

4. 我父母和我之间有代沟。(generation)

5. 他已决定退出竞赛。(withdraw from)

Reading

Out of the Wardrobe, Into a War Zone

Here in the unenchanted world of ordinary moviegoing, it has been a-bout two and a half years since "The Lion, the Witch and the Wardrobe", the first installment in Walt Disney and Walden Media's mighty "Chronicles of Narnia" franchise. In wartime England, where the Pevensie children live when they're not consorting with talking lions and battling witches, a year or so has gone by. But in Narnia itself, to which the four plucky Pevensies return in "Prince Caspian," the second movie in the series, centuries have passed, and everything has changed. The grand hall where Peter, Susan, Edmund and Lucy were made monarchs of the realm has fallen into ruin, and the friendly woodland creatures with their homey British accents and computer-animated fur seem to have vanished from the scene.

When the exiled child kings and queens are thrown back into Narnia (thanks to a sudden outbreak of special effects in a London tube station), they seem no longer to be in a children's fantasy story but rather in some kind of Jacobean tragedy, a reminder that C. S. Lewis was, along with everything else, a scholar of English Renaissance literature. In a dark castle in a dark forest, men with heavy armor and beard-shadowed faces quarrel and conspire. Instead of fauns and Turkish delight, there are murder and betrayal, and a grave, martial atmosphere lingers over the story, even when the spunky dwarfs and chatty rodents return. (Aslan the lion also shows up eventually, speaking in the soothing voice of Liam Neeson.)

So "Prince Caspian" is quite a bit darker than "The Lion, the Witch and the Wardrobe", both in look and in mood. It is also in some ways more satisfying. Its violent (though gore-free) combat scenes and high body count may rattle very young viewers, but older children are likely to be drawn into the thick political intrigue. The relative scarcity of digital effects in the first part of the movie allows the director, Andrew Adamson, and the director of photography, Karl Walter Lindenlaub, to explore the beauty of the Narnian landscape by more traditional cinematic means. Its lush glades and rocky escarpments provide a reminder that the supernaturalism of fairy tales originates in the magic of the natural world.

And tales of heroic adventure, however fanciful, are grounded in human problems of power, cruelty and conflict. "Prince Caspian" is named for its square-jawed, rather bland hero (played by Ben Barnes), but its major source of dramatic energy is the villain, Caspian's uncle Miraz, who is played with malignant grandeur by the great Italian actor Sergio Castellitto. Miraz is a classic royal usurper, who has taken the throne from Caspian's father, the rightful king, and who plans to pass it along to his own newborn son once Caspian is out of the way. His court is a viper's nest of double-dealing and shifting allegiance.

Cue grumpy dwarfs, swashbuckling mice and apple-cheeked Pevensies. And hail the popular struggle of the Narnian underground! Since the Telmarines took over and suppressed the old magic, a hardy remnant of Narnians has been hiding amid the pacified trees, sustaining themselves with the legends of King Edmund (Skandar Keynes), Queen Lucy (Georgie Henley), Queen Susan (Anna Popplewell) and High King Peter (William Moseley). When these rulers return, they rescue Trumpkin (Peter Dinklage), a small angry Narnian taken prisoner by Miraz's soldiers, and eventually join Prince Caspian, who exchanges some long, half-smoldering looks with Susan.

In spite of this hint of romance, what ensues is basically a war movie, with elaborate battle sequences in a castle courtyard and on a grassy plain, accompanied by thundering hoofbeats, whizzing arrows, clanking swords and Harry Gregson—Williams's rousing score. These sections are ostensibly what the public wants to see, and certainly what the producers pay heavily to bring to life. There is a risk of sameness and tedium, which Mr. Adamson does not entirely overcome, though he and his fellow screenwriters, Christopher Markus and Stephen McFeely, sprinkle in enough witty dialogue to keep the movie's long middle from feeling like too much of a slog.

The main characters, whose sometimes fractious sibling dynamic provided the first "Narnia" movie with a hint of psychological complexity, seem a little flatter here, as if they've grown accustomed to their jobs as action heroes. And "Prince Caspian" isn't really about them, anyway, except insofar as the kids in the audience identify with their courage and good sense.

The cloak of allegory in which Lewis swathed the Narnia books is worn lightly on the screen, and some of their charm and novelty has been chipped away — not so much by any lapse on the part of the filmmakers as by a sense of familiarity. Tales of good and evil set in enchanted lands populated by mythical beasts are ubiquitous these days, which may diminish the power of each new spell. The Pevensie children can withdraw to London between episodes, but moviegoers are unlikely, and also perhaps unwilling, to escape from Narnia and the other increasingly numerous, and therefore increasingly mundane, places like it.

New Words

franchise ['fræn₁tʃaiz]

v. grant a statutory right to a person or group by a government 赋予特权

plucky ['plʌki]

adj. having or showing gut brave 勇敢的；有胆量的

monarch ['mɔnək]	*n.* supreme ruler; king, queen, emperor or empress 最高统治者；国王、女王
realm [relm]	*n.* kingdom 王国
vanish ['væniʃ]	*v.* disappear completely and suddenly 突然完全消失
conspire [kən'spaiə]	*v.* make secret plans (with others), esp. to do wrong （与他人）密谋
faun [fɔːn]	*n.* (in Roman myths) god of the fields and woods, with goat's horns and legs but a human torso（罗马神话的）农牧神
martial ['mɑːʃəl]	*adj.* of or associated with war 战争的；军事的
rodent ['rəudənt]	*n.* type of small animal that gnaws things with its strong front teeth, e. g. a rat, squirrel or beaver 啮齿目动物（如老鼠、松鼠或海狸）
rattle ['rætl]	*v.* ①move with a sound 移动时发出嘈杂声 ②cause to make short successive sounds or annoyed 使作响；使恼火
intrigue [in'triːg]	*n.* a secret plan to do sth. bad 阴谋；密谋（做坏事）
scarcity ['skɛəsiti]	*n.* (instance of) shortage 不足；缺乏

lush [lʌʃ]

adj. growing thickly and strongly; luxuriant 繁密的；茂盛的

glade [gleid]

n. open space in a forest; clearing 森林中的空地

escarpment [isˈkɑːpmənt]

n. long steep slope or cliff separating two areas at different levels, usu. a plateau and a low-lying plain （通常为处于高低两平原之间的）长而陡的坡或悬崖

bland [blænd]

adj. gentle or casual in manner; showing no strong emotions 文雅的；随和的；不动感情的

malignant [məˈlignənt]

adj. （of people or their actions）feeling or showing great desire to harm others; malevolent （指人或人的行为）恶毒的；恶意的

viper [ˈvaipə]

n. any of various types of poisonous snake found in Africa, Asia and Europe 蝮蛇

allegiance [əˈliːdʒəns]

n. support of or loyalty to a government, ruler, cause, etc. 拥护；忠诚

grumpy [ˈgrʌmpi]

adj. bad-tempered; surly 脾气坏的；脾气暴躁的

swashbuckling [ˈswɔʃˌbʌkliŋ]

adj. typical of the exciting adventures and romantic appearance of pirates, soldiers of former times, etc. , esp. as shown in films（昔日海盗、武士等）惊险传奇式的

remnant ['remnənt]

n. small remaining quantity or part or number of things or people（事物或人）剩余的小部分；余下的数量

elaborate [i'læbəreit]

adj. very detailed and complicated; carefully prepared and finished 详尽而复杂的；精心制作的

whizzing ['wiziŋ]

adj. make a soft swishing sound 飕飕的（风声）

clanking ['klæŋkiŋ]

adj. having a hard metallic sound 叮叮当当的

rousing ['rauziŋ]

adj. vigorous; giving encouragement（esp. to action）充满活力的；激励人的

ostensibly [ɔs'tensəbli]

adv. from appearances alone 表面上地

tedium ['ti:diəm]

n. tediousness; boredom 厌倦；厌烦；乏味

sprinkle ['spriŋkl]

v. scatter or throw sth. in small drops or particles; scatter a shower of small drops, etc. on（a surface）撒某物；将某物撒在另一物的表面上

slog ［slɔg］	*n.* period of hard work or walking 艰难的工作或行走期间
fractious ［ˈfrækʃəs］	*adj.* (esp. of children) irritable; bad-tempered（尤指儿童）易怒的；脾气坏的
sibling ［ˈsibliŋ］	*n.* any one of two or more people with the same parents; brother or sister 兄弟姊妹
flatter ［ˈflætə］	*v.* praise sb. too much or insincerely, esp. in order to gain favour for oneself 恭维；奉承
cloak ［kləuk］	*n.* sleeveless outer garment hanging loosely from the shoulders 斗篷；披风
allegory ［ˈæligəri］	*n.* (style of a) story, painting or description in which the characters and events are meant as symbols of purity, truth, patience, etc. 寓言（体）；讽喻风格
swathe ［sweið］	*v.* wrap sb./sth. in several layers of bandages, warm clothes, etc. 缠绕或层层裹住
novelty ［ˈnɔvəlti］	*n.* quality of being fresh; newness; strangeness 新奇；新颖；奇异
ubiquitous ［juːˈbikwitəs］	*adj.* (seeming to be) present everywhere or in several places at the

same time 普遍存在的；无处不有的

diminish [di'miniʃ]   v. become smaller or less; decrease
变小；变少

mundane ['mʌndein]   adj. ordinary and typically unexciting 平凡的；平淡的

Phrases and Expressions

consort with：keep company with；hang out with 陪伴

fairy tales：a story about fairies，told to amuse children 童话

Reading Comprehension

Read this article carefully and answer the following questions.

1. What is the Pevensie brothers' kingdom like in this movie?

2. How do the Pevensie brothers go back to Narnia?

3. In which parts is "Prince Caspian" darker than "The Lion, the Witch, and the Wardrobe"?

4. According to the writer, what is King Miraz like?

5. What is the risk that Mr. Adamson does not entirely overcome?

Chapter Five

The Graduate

Plastics.

Main Characters

Benjamin Braddock.........................Dustin Hoffman
Mrs. Robinson............................Anne Bancroft
Elaine Robinson.........................Kathrine Ross
Mr. Robinson...........................Murray Hamilton
Mr. Braddock...........................William Daniels
Mrs. Braddock.........................Elizabeth Wilson

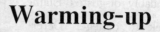

Warming-up

Synopsis

"Just one word: plastic." "Are you here for an affair?" These lines and others became cultural touchstones, as 1960s youth rebellion seeped into the California upper middle-class in Mike Nichols' landmark hit. Mentally adrift the summer after graduating from college, suburbanite Benjamin Braddock (Dustin Hoffman) would rather float in his parents' pool than follow adult advice about his future. But the exhortation

of family friend Mr. Robinson (Murray Hamilton) to seize every possible opportunity inspires Benjamin to accept an offer of sex from icily feline

Mrs. Robinson (Anne Bancroft).

The affair and the pool are all well and good until Benjamin is pushed to go out with the Robinsons' daughter Elaine (Katharine Ross) and he falls in love with her. Mrs. Robinson sabotages the relationship and an understandably disgusted Elaine runs back to college. Determined not to let Elaine get away, Benjamin follows her to school and then disrupts her family-sanctioned wedding. None too happy about her predetermined destiny, Elaine decides to flee with Benjamin.

After a violent struggle with Elaine's parents and wedding guests (Benjamin armed only with a large cross), Benjamin and Elaine escape on a public bus. The escaping couple sits smiling at the back of the bus with other passengers staring at them in mute disbelief.

The movie closes with a shot toward the back window of the bus focused on Benjamin and Elaine's smiles. As the soundtrack fades into Simon & Garfunkel, Benjamin's smile fades to an enigmatic, neutral, somewhat uncomfortable expression as he gazes forward into the bus. Elaine looks at Benjamin's expression and takes on a similar gaze.

New Words

affair [ə'fɛə]　　*n.* sexual relationship between people who are not married to each other 与配偶以外的人发生的性关系
n. things (to be) done; concern; matter 事务；事情

touchstone [ˈtʌtʃstəʊn]   *n.* a basis for comparison; a reference point against which other things can be evaluated 标准；试金石

rebellion [riˈbeljən]   *n.* open (esp. armed) resistance to the established government; resistance to authority or control 对政府的公开（尤指武装）反抗；对权威或管控的反抗

seep [siːp]   *v.* flow slowly and in small quantities through a substance（指液体）漏出、渗出

adrift [əˈdrift]   *adj.* （esp. of a boat）driven by wind and water and out of control（尤指船）失去控制而随风及水流漂浮

suburbanite [səˈbəːbənait]   *n.* a person who lives in the suburbs 郊区居民

exhortation [ˌegzɔːˈteiʃən]   *n.* an earnest attempt at persuasion 劝告

icily [ˈaisili]   *adv.* in a cold and icy manner 冷冰冰地

feline [ˈfiːlain]   *n.* animal of the cat family 猫科动物

sabotage [ˈsæbətɑːʒ]   *v.* secretly damage, destroy or spoil （sth.）阴谋破坏（某事物）

sanction [ˈsæŋkʃən]   *v.* give one's permission for sth.; authorize or approve 同意；批准

mute [mjuːt]   *adj*. silent; making no sound 沉默的；无声的

disbelief [ˈdisbiˈliːf]   *n*. lack of belief; failure to believe 不相信；怀疑

enigmatic [ˌenigˈmætik]   *adj*. difficult to understand; mysterious 难以理解的；神秘的

neutral [ˈnjuːtrəl]   *adj*. not supporting or helping either side in a dispute; impartial 中立的；不偏不倚的

gaze [geiz]   *v*. look long and steadily at sb./sth., usu. in surprise or admiration 久久地凝视、注视

Phrases and Expressions

fade into：cause to lose brightness, colour, strength, freshness, etc. 逐渐消失

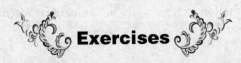

Exercises

Read the synopsis carefully and answer the following questions.

1. What is Benjamin Braddock's attitude towards life after his graduation?
2. Who coaxes Benjamin to accept an offer of sex?
3. Is Benjamin willing to go out with Elaine at the very first?
4. Does Benjamin like Elaine after their first date?
5. How does Mrs. Robinson react towards the relationship between Benjamin and Elaine?
6. Why does Elaine flee away with Benjamin in her wedding?

Scene Study

Scene 1

Mrs. Robinson successfully persuades Benjamin to drive her home and stay for a drink.

Mrs. Robinson:　Thank you.

Benjamin:　Right.

Mrs. Robinson:　Will you come in, please?

Benjamin:　What?

Mrs. Robinson:　I'd like you to come in till I get the lights on.

Benjamin:　What for?

Mrs. Robinson:　Because I don't feel safe till I get the lights on. Would you mind walking ahead of me to the sun porch? I feel funny about coming into a dark house.

Benjamin:　But it's light in there.

Mrs. Robinson:　Please. What do you drink? Bourbon?

Benjamin:　Look, Mrs. Robinson, I drove you home. I was glad to do it. But I have some things on my mind. Can you understand that?

Mrs. Robinson:　Yes. All right. What do you drink? Benjamin, I'm sorry to be this way, but I don't want to be left alone in this house.

Benjamin:　Why not?

Mrs. Robinson:　Please wait till my husband gets home.

Benjamin:　When is he coming back?

Mrs. Robinson:　I don't know. Drink?

Benjamin:　No. Are you always this much afraid of being alone?

Mrs. Robinson:	Yes.
Benjamin:	Well, why can't you just lock the doors and go to bed?
Mrs. Robinson:	I'm very neurotic. May I ask you a question? What do you think of me?
Benjamin:	What do you mean?
Mrs. Robinson:	You've known me nearly all your life. You must've formed some opinion of me.
Benjamin:	Well, I always thought that you were a very nice person.
Mrs. Robinson:	Did you know I was an alcoholic?
Benjamin:	What?
Mrs. Robinson:	Did you know that?
Benjamin:	Look, I think I should be going.
Mrs. Robinson:	Sit down, Benjamin.
Benjamin:	Mrs. Robinson, if you don't mind my saying so, this conversation is getting a little strange. Now, I'm sure Mr. Robinson will be here any minute...
Mrs. Robinson:	No.
Benjamin:	What?
Mrs. Robinson:	My husband will be back quite late. He should be gone for several hours.
Benjamin:	Oh, my god.
Mrs. Robinson:	Pardon?
Benjamin:	Oh, no, Mrs. Robinson. Oh, no.
Mrs. Robinson:	What's wrong?
Benjamin:	Mrs. Robinson, you didn't...I mean, you didn't expect...
Mrs. Robinson:	What?
Benjamin:	I mean, you didn't really think I'd do something like that.
Mrs. Robinson:	Like what? What do you think?

Benjamin:	Well, I don't know. For god's sake, Mrs. Robinson. Here we are. You got me into your house, you give me a drink, you put on music, now you start opening up your personal life to me and telling me your husband won't be home for hours.
Mrs. Robinson:	So?
Benjamin:	Mrs. Robinson, you're trying to seduce me. Aren't you?
Mrs. Robinson:	Well, no, I hadn't thought of it. I feel very flattered.
Benjamin:	Will you forgive me for what I just said?
Mrs. Robinson:	It's all right.
Benjamin:	It's not all right. It's the worst thing I ever said to anyone.
Mrs. Robinson:	Sit down.
Benjamin:	Please forgive me, because I like you. I don't think of you that way, but I'm mixed up.
Mrs. Robinson:	It's all right. Finish your drink.
Benjamin:	Mrs. Robinson, it makes me sick that I said that to you.
Mrs. Robinson:	We'll forget it right now. Finish your drink.
Benjamin:	What is wrong with me?
Mrs. Robinson:	Have you ever seen Elaine's portrait?
Benjamin:	Wha... her portrait?
Mrs. Robinson:	Yes.
Benjamin:	No.
Mrs. Robinson:	We had it done last Christmas. Would you like to see it?
Benjamin:	Very much.

New Words

porch [pɔːtʃ]

n. covered entrance to a building, esp. a church or house 门廊（尤指教堂或房子的）

Bourbon ['buəbən]

n. type of whisky distilled in the U. S. chiefly from maize 波旁威士忌

seduce [si'djuːs]

v. ① tempt (esp. sb. younger or less experienced) to have sexual intercourse 引诱（尤指年轻或无经验的人）性交 ② persuade sb. to do sth. wrong, or sth. he would not normally do, esp. by offering sth. desirable as a reward, etc. 唆使某人做坏事

flatter ['flætə]

v. praise sb. too much or insincerely, esp. in order to gain favour for oneself 恭维；奉承；讨好

portrait ['pɔːtrit]

n. painted picture, drawing or photograph of (esp. the face of) a person or an animal 人或动物的画像；（尤指面部的）肖像

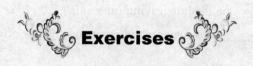

Exercises

 Comprehension of the Scene

Watch the scene carefully and answer the following questions.

1. Why would Mrs. Robinson want Benjamin to come in till she got the lights on?

2. How long would Mrs. Robinson like Benjamin to stay?

3. What did Benjamin think of Mrs. Robinson?

4. Had Benjamin known that Mrs. Robinson was an alcoholic?

5. Did Mrs. Robinson admit that she was trying to seduce Benjamin at first? Why?

6. Why did Mrs. Robinson suggest Benjamin going to see Elaine's portrait?

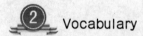 Vocabulary

Fill in the blanks with the words given below, and change the form when necessary.

portrait	alcoholic	flatter	Bourbon
conversation	seduce	porch	

1. He _____ her about her cooking.

2. In everyday _____, you request people to do things, not "order" them.

3. A pigeon perched on our _____ railing.

4. The generic term for wine, spirits and beer is _____ beverages.

5. How can I tell the difference between Scotch and _____?

6. In the _____ he is shown lying on a sofa?

7. He was _____ into leaving the company by the offer of higher pay elsewhere.

 Translation

Translate the following sentences into English，using the words given in the brackets.

1. 我是在教堂的门廊处遇到那个人的。（porch）

2. 蒙您邀请在此会上演说，我深感荣幸。（flatter）

3. 他有点神经质，但他的妻子是一个非常稳重的人。（neurotic）

4. 他最好加强自我管束，不然就会步他父亲的后尘，当一名酒鬼完结一生。（alcoholic）

5. 暖和的天气诱使我放下了学习。（seduce）

6. 他自从参加了会话班，法语取得了很大进步。（conversation）

7. 她母亲的这张肖像是她最珍爱的物品。（portrait）

Scene 2
Mrs. Robinson seduces Benjamin into Elaine's room.

Mrs. Robinson：It's here in Elaine's room.

Benjamin：Elaine certainly is an attractive girl, isn't she? I don't remember her as having brown eyes.

Mrs. Robinson：Benjamin.

Benjamin：Yes.

Mrs. Robinson：Will you come over here a minute?

Benjamin：Over there?

Mrs. Robinson：Mm Hmm.

Benjamin：Sure.

Mrs. Robinson：Will you unzip my dress? I think I'll go to bed.

Benjamin：Oh, well, good night.

Mrs. Robinson：Won't you unzip my dress?

Benjamin:	I'd rather not, Mrs. Robinson.
Mrs. Robinson:	If you still think I'm trying to seduce you...
Benjamin:	No, I don't, but I just feel a little funny.
Mrs. Robinson:	Benjamin, you've known me all your life.
Benjamin:	I know that, but I'm...
Mrs. Robinson:	Come on, it's hard for me to reach. Thank you.
Benjamin:	Right.
Mrs. Robinson:	What are you so scared of?
Benjamin:	I'm not scared, Mrs. Robinson.
Mrs. Robinson:	Then why do you keep running away?
Benjamin:	Because you're going to bed. I don't think I should be up here.
Mrs. Robinson:	Haven't you seen anybody in a slip before?
Benjamin:	Yes, I have, but I just... Look, what if Mr. Robinson walked in right now?
Mrs. Robinson:	What if he did?
Benjamin:	Well. It would look pretty funny, wouldn't it?
Mrs. Robinson:	Don't you think he'd trust us together?
Benjamin:	Of course, he does, but he might get the wrong idea. Anyone might.
Mrs. Robinson:	I don't see why. I'm twice as old as you. How could anyone think...
Benjamin:	They would, don't you see?
Mrs. Robinson:	Benjamin, I am not trying to seduce you.
Benjamin:	I know that, but please, Mrs. Robinson, this is difficult...
Mrs. Robinson:	Would you like me to seduce you?
Benjamin:	What?
Mrs. Robinson:	Is that what you're trying to tell me?
Benjamin:	I'm going home now. I apologize for what I said. I hope you can forget it, but I'm going home right now.

Mrs. Robinson：	Benjamin.
Benjamin：	Yes?
Mrs. Robinson：	Will you bring up my purse before you go?
Benjamin：	I have to go now. I'm sorry.
Mrs. Robinson：	I really don't want to put this on again. Won't you bring it up?
Benjamin：	Where is it?
Mrs. Robinson：	On the table in the hall.
Benjamin：	Mrs. Robinson?
Mrs. Robinson：	I'm in the bathroom.
Benjamin：	Well，here's the purse.
Mrs. Robinson：	Could you bring it up?
Benjamin：	Well，I'll hand it to you. Come to the railing, and I'll hand it up.
Mrs. Robinson：	Benjamin, I'm getting pretty tired of all the suspicion. Now, if you won't do me a simple favor, I don't know what.
Benjamin：	I'm putting it on the top step.
Mrs. Robinson：	For god's sake，Benjamin，will you stop acting this way and bring me the purse?
Benjamin：	I'm putting it here by the door.
Mrs. Robinson：	Will you bring it in to me?
Benjamin：	I'd rather not.
Mrs. Robinson：	All right. Put it in Elaine's room where we were.
Benjamin：	Right. Oh, god. Oh, let me out.
Mrs. Robinson：	Don't be nervous.
Benjamin：	Get away from that door.
Mrs. Robinson：	I want to say something first.
Benjamin：	Jesus Christ.
Mrs. Robinson：	Benjamin, I want you to know that I'm available to you, and if you won't sleep with me this time. . .

Benjamin:	Oh, my Christ.
Mrs. Robinson:	If you won't sleep with me this time, I want you to know you can call me up anytime, and we'll make some kind of an arrangement. Do you understand what I'm saying?
Benjamin:	Let me out.
Mrs. Robinson:	Benjamin, do you understand?
Benjamin:	Yes, yes, let me out.
Mrs. Robinson:	I find you very attractive. And tell me what...
Benjamin:	Oh, Jesus, that's him!

New Words

unzip [ʌnˈzip]	v. open the zipper of 拉开拉链
slip [slip]	n. act of moving smoothly; false step 滑动；失足
railing [ˈreiliŋ]	n. a barrier consisting of a horizontal bar 横条的栏杆

Phrases and Expressions

be scared of: full of fear; frightened 害怕

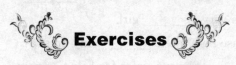

Exercises

Comprehension of the Scene

Judge whether the following statements are TRUE or FALSE.

1. Mrs. Robinson asked Benjamin to unzip for her because she really wanted to go to bed.

2. Benjamin refused to unzip Mrs. Robinson's dress at the very beginning.

3. Pretending to be calm, Benjamin was very scared that Mr. Robinson appeared suddenly.

4. Since Mrs. Robinson was twice as old as Benjamin, it's impossible for her to have an affair with him.

5. When asking Benjamin to bring her purse, Mrs. Robinson's real purpose was still seducing him.

6. Mrs. Robinson promised Benjamin that she was always available to him.

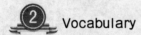 Vocabulary

Fill in the blanks with the words given below, and change the form when necessary.

apologize	available	be scared of	arrangement
railing	attractive	unzip	suspicion

1. Don't _____ the supervisor. His bark is worse than his bite and he's really a nice guy.

2. We have made all the _____ for the conference.

3. You will be informed when the book becomes _____.

4. The talks have resulted in a lessening of _____.

5. I think she is a very _____ girl.

6. Could you please help me to _____ my dress?

7. You must _____ to your sister for being so rude.

8. The space around the altar of a church for the clergy and sometimes the choir is often enclosed by a lattice or _____.

Translation

Translate the following sentences into English，using the words or expressions given in the brackets.

1. 这孩子害怕那条外表凶恶的狗。(be scared of)

2. 在这个价格范围内，有好几种汽车可供选购。(available)

3. 他们有一种令人不安的猜疑，所有的事都不太妙。(suspicion)

4. 冰激凌对孩子们非常有吸引力。(attractive)

5. 你应该讲点礼貌，为你所做的事道歉。(apologize)

6. 他跌了一跤，头部撞在栏杆上了。(railing)

Scene 3
Benjamin finally plucked enough courage to ask Mrs. Robinson to come to the Taft Hotel.

Mrs. Robinson：	Hello，Benjamin.
Benjamin：	Hello，Mrs. Robinson.
Mrs. Robinson：	Well.
Benjamin：	Well.
Mrs. Robinson：	Benjamin...
Benjamin：	Yes.
Mrs. Robinson：	I'll get undressed now. Is that all right?
Benjamin：	Sure. Shall I...I mean, should I just stand here? I mean, I don't know what you want me to do.
Mrs. Robinson：	Why don't you watch?
Benjamin：	Oh, sure. Thank you.
Mrs. Robinson：	Will you bring me a hanger?
Benjamin：	What?
Mrs. Robinson：	A hanger.
Benjamin：	Oh, yes. Wood?
Mrs. Robinson：	What?

Benjamin:	Wood or wire? They have both.
Mrs. Robinson:	Either one would be fine.
Benjamin:	OK.
Mrs. Robinson:	Thank you. Would you help me with this, please?
Benjamin:	Certainly.
Mrs. Robinson:	Thank you.
Benjamin:	You're welcome.
Mrs. Robinson:	Benjamin, would this be easier for you in the dark?
Benjamin:	Mrs. Robinson, I can't do this.
Mrs. Robinson:	You what?
Benjamin:	This is all terribly wrong.
Mrs. Robinson:	Do you find me undesirable?
Benjamin:	Oh, no, Mrs. Robinson. I think you're the most attractive of all my parents' friends. I mean that. I find you desirable, but I... For god's sake, can you imagine my parents? Can you imagine what they'd say if they just saw us here in this room right now?
Mrs. Robinson:	What would they say?
Benjamin:	I have no idea, Mrs. Robinson, but for god's sake, they brought me up. They made a good life for me, and I think they deserve better than this. I think they deserve a little better than jumping into bed with the partner's wife.
Mrs. Robinson:	Are you afraid of me?
Benjamin:	Oh, no, you're missing the point. Look, maybe we could do something else together. Mrs. Robinson, would you like to go to a movie?
Mrs. Robinson:	Can I ask you a personal question?
Benjamin:	Ask me anything you want.
Mrs. Robinson:	Is this your first time?
Benjamin:	Is this what?

Mrs. Robinson:	It is, isn't it? It is your first time.
Benjamin:	That's a laugh, Mrs. Robinson. That's really a laugh.
Mrs. Robinson:	Well, you can admit that, can't you?
Benjamin:	Are you kidding?
Mrs. Robinson:	It's nothing to be ashamed of.
Benjamin:	Wait a minute.
Mrs. Robinson:	On your first time...
Benjamin:	Who said it was my first time? Wait a minute.
Mrs. Robinson:	Just because you happen to be inadequate in one way.
Benjamin:	Inadequate?
Mrs. Robinson:	Well, I guess I better...
Benjamin:	Don't move!

New Words

undressed ['ʌn'drest]　　　*adj.* with one's clothes off; naked 已脱掉衣物的；裸露的

hanger ['hæŋə]　　　*n.* ①loop or hook on or by which sth. is hung（挂东西的）环、挂钩 ②a person who tries to become or appear friendly with others, esp. in the hope of personal gain 竭力讨好他人的人

desirable [di'zaiərəbl]　　　*adj.* ① (of a person) arousing sexual desire（指人）引起性欲的 ② worth having; to be wished for 值得有的；合意的

inadequate [in'ædikwit]　　　*adj.* ①not sufficiently able or confident to deal with a difficult situation 不足胜任的；信心不足的②not sufficient or enough; not good enough for a particular purpose 不充分的；不足的

Phrases and Expressions

be ashamed of：feeling shame or guilt because of sth. done 感到羞愧

in one way：somewhat，in some sense 稍微；在某点上

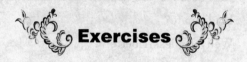 **Exercises**

 Comprehension of the Scene

Watch the scene carefully and choose the best answer.

1. When Mrs. Robinson started to get undressed，Benjamin was _____.

    A. nervous   B. excited   C. indifferent   D. happy

2. Mrs. Robinson would like Benjamin to bring her a _____.

    A. piece of wood   B. hanger

    C. cup of coffee   D. cigarette

3. Benjamin suddenly lost heart and said "This is terribly wrong"，because _____.

    A. he suddenly found Mrs. Robinson undesirable

    B. he thought Mrs. Robinson was too good for him

    C. he suddenly thought about his parents

    D. Mr. Robinson suddenly came into his mind

4. When Benjamin kept talking about his parents, he was actually _____.

    A. just too excited

    B. trying to make a decision not to sleep with Mrs. Robinson

    C. trying to persuade Mrs. Robinson to give up

D. struggling with himself whether to do it or not

5. Benjamin finally slept with Mrs. Robinson，because _____.

　A. he put his parents behind

　B. he can't help doing so

　C. Mrs. Robinson's question infuriated him

　D. Mrs. Robinson begged him to do so

 Vocabulary

Fill in the blanks with words or phrases from the scene you have just seen that match the meanings in the column on the right.

_____ of or belonging to a particular person rather than a group or an organization

_____ of a kind not to be welcomed in society; objectionable

_____ somewhat, in some sense

_____ with one's clothes off; naked

_____ feeling shame or guilt because of sth. done

_____ not sufficiently able or confident to deal with a diffi-cult situation

_____ (of a person) arousing sexual desire

_____ loop or hook on or by which sth. is hung

 Translation

Translate the following sentences into English，using the words or expressions given in the brackets.

1. 孩子脱掉衣服上床睡觉。（undressed）

2. 还有一件事，我还需要两三个衣架。（hanger）

3. 让他在这里工作其实并没必要。（desirable）

4. 这种药没有什么不良的副作用。（undesirable）

5. 我有点私事和你商量。（personal）

6. 食物不足会影响儿童的发育。(inadequate)

7. 我怎么也不会想跳进这冰冷的水里。(jump into)

8. 你应为自己所做的事感到羞愧。(be ashamed of)

9. 这些变化从某种意义上说是一种进步。(in one way)

Scene 4

Benjamin suggests that he and Mrs. Robinson should have a conversation for a change.

Benjamin：　Will you wait a minute, please? Mrs. Robinson, do you think we could say a few words to each other first this time?

Mrs. Robinson：　I don't think we have much to say to each other.

Benjamin：　Look, for months, all we've done is come up here and leap into bed together.

Mrs. Robinson：　Are you tired of it?

Benjamin：　I'm not, no. But do you think we could liven it up with a little conversation for a change?

Mrs. Robinson：　Well, what do you want to talk about?

Benjamin：　Anything. Anything at all.

Mrs. Robinson：　Do you want to tell me about some of your college experiences?

Benjamin：　Oh, my god. Think of another topic.

Mrs. Robinson：　How about art?

Benjamin：　Art. That's a good subject. You start it off.

Mrs. Robinson：　You start it off. I don't know anything about it.

Benjamin：　Well, what do you want to know about it? Are you interested more in modern art or in classical art?

Mrs. Robinson：　Neither.

Benjamin：　You're not interested in art?

Mrs. Robinson：　No.

Benjamin：　Then why do you want to talk about it?

Mrs. Robinson:	I don't.
Benjamin:	Now, look, we're going to do this thing. We're going to have a conversation. Tell me what you did today.
Mrs. Robinson:	I got up. I fixed breakfast for my husband.
Benjamin:	There. There's something we could have a conversation about your husband.
Mrs. Robinson:	Oh. Him.
Benjamin:	I mean, everything. I don't know anything about how you work this. What do you say to him when you leave the house at night?
Mrs. Robinson:	Nothing. He's asleep.
Benjamin:	Always? Doesn't he wake up when you come home?
Mrs. Robinson:	We have separate bedrooms.
Benjamin:	Oh, I see. So you don't... I don't like to seem like I'm prying, but I guess you don't sleep together anything.
Mrs. Robinson:	No, we don't.
Benjamin:	How long has this been going on?
Mrs. Robinson:	For god's sake, let's drop this.
Benjamin:	Wait a minute. Why did you marry him?
Mrs. Robinson:	See if you can guess.
Benjamin:	Well, I can't.
Mrs. Robinson:	Think real hard, Benjamin.
Benjamin:	I can't see why you did, unless... you didn't have to marry him or anything, did you?
Mrs. Robinson:	Don't tell Elaine.
Benjamin:	Oh, no. You had to marry him because you got pregnant.
Mrs. Robinson:	Are you shocked?
Benjamin:	I never thought of you and Mr. Robinson as the kind of people who...
Mrs. Robinson:	All right now, let's get to bed.

Benjamin:	Wait a minute. Wait a minute. So how did it happen?
Mrs. Robinson:	What?
Benjamin:	You and Mr. Robinson. I mean, do you feel like telling me what were the circumstances?
Mrs. Robinson:	Not particularly.
Benjamin:	Was he a law student at the time?
Mrs. Robinson:	Mm-hmm.
Benjamin:	And you were a student also?
Mrs. Robinson:	Mm-hmm.
Benjamin:	At college?
Mrs. Robinson:	Yes.
Benjamin:	What was your major?
Mrs. Robinson:	Benjamin, why are you asking me all these questions?
Benjamin:	Because I'm interested, Mrs. Robinson. What was your major subject at college?
Mrs. Robinson:	Art.
Benjamin:	Art? But I thought you... I guess you kind of lost interest in it over the years, then.
Mrs. Robinson:	Kind of.

New Words

leap [li:p]	v. jump vigorously 跳；跳跃
pry [prai]	v. inquire too curiously or rudely about other people's private affairs 打听；刺探
pregnant ['pregnant]	adj. (of a woman or female animal) having a baby or young animal developing in the womb 怀孕的；妊娠的

circumstance [ˈsəːkəmstəns]   *n.* condition or fact connected with an event or action 环境；情形

Phrases and Expressions

start off：send off 开始；出发

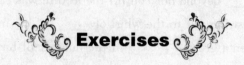
Exercises

 Comprehension of the Scene

Watch the scene carefully and answer the following questions.

1. Why did Benjamin suggest to have a conversation?
2. Was Mrs. Robinson willing to talk?
3. What was the first topic coming into Benjamin's mind?
4. What was Mrs. Robinson's major in college? And what was her husband's?
5. Why did Mrs. Robinson get married?
6. Was Mrs. Robinson still interested in art?

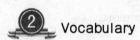 Vocabulary

Fill in the blanks with the words given below，and change the form when necessary.

classical	start off	pregnant	particular
circumstance	pry	leap	modern

1. The house itself is not _____ to my mind, but I like its environment.
2. We can make it if we _____ now.

3. She got _____ without being married and was turned out of the house by her parents.

4. I don't want them _____ into my affairs.

5. Some young people like pop music, while still others like _____ music.

6. Due to _____ beyond our control the lecture was cancelled.

7. He can't adjust himself to the whirl of _____ life in this big city.

8. There has been a great _____ in the number of births in these past five years.

 Oral Practice

What are true things about Mrs. Robinson? Tick the right answers.

1. She didn't know anything about art.

2. She was very interested in modern art.

3. She had been majored in art when she was a college student.

4. She got married with Mr. Robinson only because she loved him so much.

5. She had to marry Mr. Robinson because she was pregnant.

6. She didn't sleep together with Mr. Robinson any more.

7. She missed her daughter Elaine very much.

8. She thought law was more interesting than other subjects for college students.

Scene 5

Benjamin is asked by Elaine to go to the Taft Hotel for some drinks.

Elaine: Would you like to come in? I could make you some coffee.

Benjamin: No. I wouldn't want to wake anyone up.

Elaine: We won't. Let's go inside.

Benjamin: Wait a minute.

Elaine: Is anything wrong?

Benjamin: No. I was just thinking. It's still early. Maybe we could do something, go somewhere else.

Elaine: All right. Where are we going?

Benjamin: I'm trying to think of where there's a place to have a drink around here.

Elaine: Isn't there one at the Taft hotel? What is the matter?

Benjamin: Nothing. I'm just wondering if they have a bar or not. I mean, let's go see. Let's go see if they do or not. Listen, Elaine, it seems to me that there isn't a bar here. I mean, as far as I know.

Elaine: Of course there is. Look, there's the palm room right there.

A: Good evening.

B: Hello.

C: How are you, sir?

D: Good evening, Mr. Gladstone.

E: Hello again.

F: Hi, Mr. Gladstone. How are you this evening?

Elaine: Benjamin?

Benjamin: Let's get out of here, Elaine. Let's go somewhere else.

Elaine: Do they know you?

Benjamin: Of course not.

G: Good evening, sir.

Benjamin: Come on, Elaine, we're leaving.

H: Mr. Gladstone, how are you?

Elaine: Benjamin, what's happening?

Benjamin: I don't know. They must think I look like this guy Gladstone.

I: Hello, Mr. Braniff.

Benjamin: Elaine, I like you. I like you so much. Do you believe that? Do you?

Elaine: Yes.

Benjamin: You're the first... you're the first thing for so long that I've liked, the first person I could stand to be with. My whole life is such a waste. It's just nothing. I'm sorry. I'll take you home now.

Elaine: Benjamin, are you having an affair with someone? I'm sorry. I'm sorry. That's not my business.

Benjamin: It just happened. It's just this thing that happened along with everything else. Can you understand that?

Elaine: Was she married or something?

Benjamin: Yes.

Elaine: With a family?

Benjamin: Yes. She had a husband and a son.

Elaine: Did they ever find out?

Benjamin: No.

Elaine: And it's all over now?

Benjamin: Yes.

Elaine: I'm glad.

Benjamin: Can we do something tomorrow?

Elaine: All right.

Benjamin: During the day we'll go for a drive or something.

Elaine: OK.

Benjamin: You sure you really want to?

Elaine: Yes.

Benjamin: Because I wouldn't want you to do it unless you really wanted to.

Elaine: I do.

Benjamin: You do?

Elaine: Benjamin, I really do.

Benjamin: Shh!

New Words

palm [pɑːm] n. ① inner surface of the hand between the wrist and the fingers 掌；手掌 ② (also palm-tree) any of several types of tree growing in warm or tropical climates, with no branches and a mass of large wide leaves at the top 棕榈树

Phrases and Expressions

wake sb. up：cause sb. to become awake or conscious 叫醒某人

find out：get to know or become aware of, usually accidentally 找出；认识到

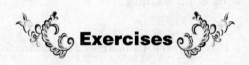 Exercises

 Comprehension of the Scene

Watch the scene carefully and judge whether the following statements are TRUE or FALSE.

1. Benjamin didn't want to come into Elaine's house because he was afraid to wake someone up.

2. When Elaine proposed to go to the Taft hotel for some drink, Benjamin was very nervous.

3. Many people in the hotel knew Benjamin, because he went there frequently with Mrs. Robinson.

4. Benjamin would like people to call him Mr. Gladstone, because he thought this name was very attractive.

5. Benjamin admitted that he had an affair with a married woman.

6. Elaine thought that Benjamin's whole life was such a waste.

7. Elaine was glad to hear that Benjamin's affair with the married woman was over.

8. Benjamin lied to Elaine by saying "She had a husband and a son", because he was afraid that Elaine may make out who he was talking about.

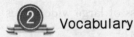 Vocabulary

Translate the following sentences, paying special attention to the underlined words and see the different meanings and usage of them.

1. **wonder**

   A. I was just underlining about that myself.

   A. I was just <u>wondering</u> about that myself.

   B. They stared at the strange sight in silent <u>wonder</u>.

   C. They <u>wondered</u> at his learning.

2. **palm**

   A. There were two or three <u>palm</u> trees flourishing in the promenade garden.

   B. He knew the passage like the <u>palm</u> of his hand.

3. **stand**

   A. My nerves won't <u>stand</u> the strain much longer.

   B. She was too weak to <u>stand</u>.

   C. I bought the newspaper from a <u>stand</u> on the road.

4. **waste**

   A. Dustbins are used for household <u>waste</u>.

   B. It's only a <u>waste</u> of time to speak to her.

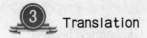 Translation

Translate the following sentences into Chinese.

1. No. I wouldn't want to wake anyone up.

2. I'm trying to think of... where there's a place to have a drink around here.

3. I'm just wondering if they have a bar or not.

4. They must think I look like this guy Gladstone.

5. You're the first thing for so long that I've liked，the first person I could stand to be with.

6. It's just this thing that happened along with everything else.

7. Because I wouldn't want you to do it unless you really wanted to.

Reading

Review

The Graduate has become a sort of rite of passage over the years. Those students getting far enough in college that they can see the light at the end of the tunnel are handed the keys to this little film to see what life has in store for them... well not entirely. For those of us who were approaching the tunnel, not knowing what to expect on the other side, or not being ready for the other side, *The Graduate* seems to have become a movie of identification even after almost 40 years.

On one level this movie is about Benjamin achieving his independence. He is struggling to become his own person and make his own decisions apart from what his parents have laid out for him. Attending graduate school was not his choice, nor does finding a job. When he is told that he can't see Elaine, it becomes his goal. She is his youthful identification but more than that she is the forbidden fruit. Both of her parents forbid Benjamin to see her. They tell him, in fact, that she will soon be married and it becomes his battle to win her back.

But on a more interesting level is Mrs. Robinson's quest for her lost youth. Often we see her as smooth and in control of the situations around her. Why wouldn't she be? Benjamin is completely lost. Her angle in the affair seems to be straightforward at first. She admits that she is attracted to Benjamin and it appears that she is unhappy with her alcoholic husband. The scene where they are in bed together chatting she begins to reveal more about her background. She almost falls into a trance when talking about her life in college before she was married. Benjamin also finds out that she and Mr. Robinson sleep in different beds and that more interestingly she conceived Elaine when she was rather young. To her, the flings with Benjamin are a source of rejuvenation. Mrs. Robinson is getting back in touch with her lost. She is unhappy with her life and her husband, and Benjamin provides her only escape.

When the idea of Benjamin and Elaine comes into the picture, Mrs. Robinson lashes out at Benjamin. Why? Benjamin claims it's because she thinks Elaine is too good for him. This is not the case. The Braddocks and the Robinsons are obviously close. The real reason is because Mrs. Robinson doesn't want to come to the realization that she is no longer a girl in her 20s.

The final scene is a great wrap to the movie. I watched this with a friend once who was livid when they got on the bus and just sat there. No hugs, no kiss. After the adrenaline fades, they sit there like an old couple who have grown apart from each other. They smile a little bit, look ahead and look around, but never at each other. Elaine and Benjamin seem a bit lost after their glorious exit from the marriage. But where do they go from there? They don't know. I saw an interview with Mike Nichols, the director of *The Graduate*, and he was asked, where he thought Elaine and Benjamin would go from there if they got married? He said they will probably end up just like their parents. So much for their youthful revolution. But you can tell by the looks on their faces on that final scene that if they stay with each other they probably have no alternative.

New Words

rite [rait]   *n.* religious or some other solemn
                                          ceremony（宗教等的）隆重的仪式
                                          或典礼

straightforward [streit'fɔ:wəd]   *adj.* honest and frank, without e-

	vasion 诚实的；坦率的
trance [trɑːns]	*n.* sleep-like state 昏睡状态
fling [fliŋ]	*n.* short period of enjoyment in some（often irresponsible）activity 一时的（常为放纵的）行乐
rejuvenation [riˈdʒuːvineiʃən]	*n.* the phenomenon of vitality and freshness being restored 恢复活力
wrap [ræp]	*n.* outer garment，e.g. a scarf, shawl or cloak 罩在外面的衣物（如围巾、披肩或斗篷）
livid [ˈlivid]	*adj.* furiously angry 大怒的
adrenaline [əˈdrenəlin]	*n.* a catecholamine secreted by the adrenal medulla in response to stress（trade name Adrenalin）；stimulates autonomic nerve action 肾上腺素
glorious [ˈɡlɔːriəs]	*adj.* having, worthy of or bringing great fame or glory 荣誉的；光荣的
alternative [ɔːlˈtəːnətiv]	*n.* a choice of two or more possibilities 可能性中的选择

Phrases and Expressions

in store：in readiness；awaiting 必将到来；快要发生

lash out：beat severely with a whip 痛打

Reading Comprehension

Read this article carefully and answer the following questions.

1. What is Benjamin struggling for in this movie?

2. In the author's opinion, why does Benjamin try so hard to get Elaine?

3. According to the author, why does Mrs. Robinson seduce Benjamin? Does she really love him?

4. Why does Mrs. Robinson outraged at thinking that Benjamin and Elaine may be together?

5. What does the last scene of the movie indicate?

图书在版编目（CIP）数据

新视角电影英语．成长篇/罗振宁，谭慧主编．—北京：
中国电影出版社，2011.10
ISBN 978-7-106-03043-8

Ⅰ．新… Ⅱ.①罗… ②谭… Ⅲ．电影—英语—
教材 Ⅳ.H31

中国版本图书馆 CIP 数据核字（2009）第 033762 号

策　　划：崔　巍
责任编辑：崔　巍
书籍设计：张　爽
责任校对：魏晓峰
责任印制：张玉民

新视角电影英语　成长篇

罗振宁　谭　慧　主编

出版发行　中国电影出版社（北京北三环东路 22 号）邮编 100013
　　　　　电话：64296664（总编室）　 64216278（发行部）
　　　　　　　　64296742（读者服务部）　Email：cfpygb@126.com
经　　销　新华书店
印　　刷　北京鑫丰华彩印有限公司
版　　次　2011 年 10 月第 1 版　2011 年 10 月北京第 1 次印刷
规　　格　开本/787 × 1092 毫米　1/16
　　　　　印张/12.25　　插页/2　　字数/301 千字
印　　数　1 - 2000 册

书　　号　ISBN 978-7-106-03043-8/H・0009
定　　价　30.00 元